P9-DHS-497

GHOSTS of WAR
The Secret of Midway

STEVE WATKINS

SCHOLASTIC INC.

Copyright © 2015 by Steve Watkins

If you purchased this book without a cover, you should be aware that this book is stolen property. It was reported as "unsold and destroyed" to the publisher, and neither the author nor the publisher has received any payment for this "stripped book."

No part of this publication may be reproduced, stored in a retrieval system, or transmitted in any form or by any means, electronic, mechanical, photocopying, recording, or otherwise, without written permission of the publisher. For information regarding permission, write to Scholastic Inc., Attention: Permissions Department, 557 Broadway, New York, NY 10012.

All rights reserved. Published by Scholastic Inc. SCHOLASTIC and associated logos are trademarks and/or registered trademarks of Scholastic Inc.

ISBN 978-0-545-66585-8

12 11 10 9 8 7 6 5 4 3 2 1   15 16 17 18 19 20/0

Printed in the U.S.A.   40
First printing, January 2015
Book design by Yaffa Jaskoll

For Lili and Claire

I had a big favor to ask my uncle Dex, but first I had to listen to him tell me for about the millionth time all about the Civil War Battle of Fredericksburg. That's the town where we live in Virginia. Uncle Dex is really into history and so am I, though I don't make a big deal about it. Especially to my best friend, Greg Troutman, because he hates school more than anybody on the planet.

We'd been studying the Battle of Fredericksburg in our sixth-grade history class, and I'd made the mistake of mentioning that to Uncle Dex. I was warming up to asking him if we could use some space in his store for our band to practice.

"The Union should have won that battle," he said. "Did

you learn that in history class, Anderson? All the Union had to do was cross the river into town. The Confederates weren't even there yet. If they could have just crossed the river, the Yankees would have taken Fredericksburg and then marched on through Virginia into Richmond and probably ended the war a couple of years early. If only they'd had a bridge."

We were in Uncle Dex's junk shop downtown where he sold all sorts of vintage stuff and antiques and odds and ends. It used to belong to my grandpa, Pop Pop. Uncle Dex took it over last year after Pop Pop died. The actual name of the store is "The Kitchen Sink," which is supposed to mean it has everything you might ever want, but Uncle Dex ends up having to explain what's in there because most people think it's a hardware store.

Uncle Dex jabbered on for a while longer about how the Yankees took too long getting pontoons down from Washington to make their own bridge, so Robert E. Lee had time to move the Confederate troops into position. And then when the Yankees finally crossed over the river, they got slaughtered.

"You know what Robert E. Lee said after the Battle of Fredericksburg, don't you?" he said, hopefully winding down the history lesson. "It's a pretty famous saying."

I scratched my head, to show him I was seriously thinking

about it, only I had on a beanie, so mostly I just moved the beanie back and forth. Greg said we should wear them to make us look cooler. I didn't know if it was working, but when you're invisible at school and trying to start up a band, you need all the help you can get.

"I guess not," I said.

Uncle Dex straightened his baseball cap, lifted his hand, stuck out his index finger, and began quoting Robert E. Lee: "It is well that *war is so terrible*, otherwise we should grow too fond of it."

"Right," I said, not really sure what that was supposed to mean. I'd have to think about it later. For now, though, on to business.

"So, Uncle Dex," I said, "I was wondering if maybe you might have some space in the shop's basement, a room or something, where we could practice with our band?"

The Kitchen Sink basement isn't just one room. It's like the Roman catacombs, so I figured there must be plenty of empty rooms that Uncle Dex wouldn't mind us using. And the farther away from anywhere people could hear us, the better — at least until we learned a few songs all the way through, and maybe some more chords.

Uncle Dex looked very serious all of a sudden. "A band?"

I nodded. "Yep. A band. Me and Greg. We both play the guitar. Well, I'm on rhythm guitar."

Uncle Dex looked even more serious. And he started nodding. "So you probably need a keyboard player," he said. "Like me."

I didn't know what to say. He'd caught me off guard. Was he seriously asking if he could be in the band? A grown-up?

"You know I used to play, right?" he said. "When I was in high school. We had a band, too. Plus, in college I was in a ukulele ensemble."

"I'm not in high school yet," I said, as if that was the real issue here. "I'm just in sixth grade. And anyway, we kind of already have a keyboard player." That was a lie, but I had to say something.

"Oh yeah?" he said, as if he didn't quite believe me.

"Yeah," I said. "A girl, actually." I blurted that out without thinking about it, although a girl had, in fact, asked me and Greg if she could be in the band. Her name was Julie Kobayashi and we hadn't ever talked to her much, even though she'd been around since elementary school. She'd overheard us talking about our plans to write some songs and perform them at one of the All-Ages Open Mic Nights they had at this big warehouse downtown.

Of course, we'd told Julie Kobayashi no. We didn't want a girl in the band, and especially a girl like Julie, who was probably even more invisible than me and Greg. With that much invisibility onstage, it would be as if we weren't even there.

Not that Uncle Dex had to know any of that.

"Well, okay then," he said. "But, hey, if you need a ukulele, I'm your guy."

"Definitely," I said, meaning "definitely not."

Uncle Dex led me down to the basement, then through a confusing series of hallways until he suddenly stopped. "In here," he said, tapping on a green door. "There's just some of Pop Pop's old stuff he bought at yard sales in this one. Clear it out and the space is yours." He winked at me, which is a thing only grown-ups ever do.

We both had to pull hard to get the door open. It made one of those haunted mansion sounds that sends chills up your spine. Then we had to wade through a bunch of cobwebs to get inside, though we couldn't go very far. A mountain of stuff was piled up everywhere.

Uncle Dex patted me on the back — another thing only grown-ups ever do — and then headed back upstairs to see if any actual human customers had wandered into the store.

I just stood there, frozen, overwhelmed by the amount of work it was going to take to even make a pig path through all that junk. I was also totally creeped out. I definitely had the feeling that I wasn't alone.

I pulled out my cell phone so I could text Greg. We'd ridden our bikes downtown, but he was off wandering around somewhere while I talked to Uncle Dex. I couldn't get a signal, though. Sometimes that happens. But sometimes if I lift the phone up over my head, I'll get lucky.

So that's what I was doing, waving my cell phone around, when a cold hand clamped down on my shoulder.

I screamed, and then dove forward to get away from whatever it was, crashing into an enormous pile of boxes that came tumbling down on top of me.

"Help!" I yelled — because of the hand and because now I was totally buried.

Somebody started pulling boxes off me — but I had a panicky feeling that it wasn't Uncle Dex.

"Did you wet your pants, Anderson?" a familiar voice asked, and then burst out laughing, or rather, snorting.

It wasn't Uncle Dex, as it turned out, and it wasn't a ghost, either.

It was my moron best friend.

I yelled at Greg for a while

for scaring me so bad, but it didn't bother him. I don't think he even heard half of what I said because of all his laughing.

When I finally calmed down and climbed out, and he finally quit snorting, I told him everything and we got to work clearing out Uncle Dex's dungeon. It took us the rest of the afternoon. Mostly we just stacked boxes higher and higher up against the walls, which might have been kind of dangerous, but we didn't know what else to do with them. We dragged a bunch down the hall to some other rooms also jammed with boxes and shoved the new ones in wherever we could find space.

I had to keep rubbing my eyes, and Greg sneezed his head off the whole time.

"I probably won't be able to go to school tomorrow because of my allergies," he said, sounding almost happy. "And by the way, your eyes are so red, you probably ruptured all the capillaries or veins or whatever. You should probably stay home, too. Maybe we can hang out."

"I wish," I said. If it was just my mom I might be able to fake sick, but Dad thought a perfect attendance record was more important than, well, anything. I hadn't missed a day of school since I had to get my tonsils out in kindergarten. And even then, Dad tried to convince Mom that I should just take an aspirin and go.

One weird thing about clearing out all those boxes and junk was that there was this one beat-up wooden chest or footlocker or something that neither one of us would touch. We didn't avoid it exactly, just sort of worked around the edges until it was sitting there all alone right in the middle of the room. It creeped me out for some reason, the same way the whole room had creeped me out when Uncle Dex first left.

Greg and I both acted like it wasn't even there. I figured if I didn't say anything and ignored it, he would haul it off or whatever. As it turned out, he must have been thinking the same thing.

"Well," I said finally, at about six o'clock. "That just about does it."

Greg stopped what he was doing and stood beside me. We surveyed the room, or the middle of it, where we'd cleared enough stuff away that we'd probably have space for us and our guitars and our amplifiers, which weren't that big.

There still wasn't any mention of the trunk.

"So your uncle," Greg said. "He really wants to be in the band?"

"That's what he said," I replied. "But who knows. He's kind of weird and was probably just kidding around." The truth was you really couldn't be too sure with Uncle Dex.

Greg grunted as he lifted one last box up onto an already shaky pile. I was too tired to help, so I just watched him drag it up there.

"I could use a hand here!" he yelled at me as he struggled with the box.

"Okay," I said, and started clapping. He actually growled.

He climbed back down from the pile of boxes and sat down on the floor next to me. I thought maybe he would punch me on the arm, but he brought up the band again instead.

"Are we going to have to let that girl in?" he asked. "Julie Kobayashi. Since you told your uncle she's playing keyboard?"

I groaned. I'd forgotten about her. Uncle Dex was gonna know we didn't have a keyboard player if Julie wasn't coming to practices at the shop.

"My brain's tired," I said. "We'll figure it out later."

Greg shrugged. "Okay with me," he said, and stood up to leave.

I started to follow, but found myself taking one last look at the wooden trunk. It might have been just my imagination, but there seemed to be a faint golden glow around it. Kind of a shimmering light.

I rubbed my eyes one more time and looked again, but this time there was nothing. Probably it had just been the last light of the day coming in from this one high basement window about twelve feet up.

Greg was already halfway up the stairs, so I hurried to catch up. Uncle Dex was gone when we got upstairs. He'd turned off all the lights, probably forgetting we were still down in the basement all that time.

"Man, is this spooky or what?" Greg said.

"Yeah," I answered. "Let's get out of here."

The only problem was that a key was needed to lock the store — which Uncle Dex must have forgotten.

"What now?" Greg asked.

I was tired and dirty from all that work, and wanted to just say that if Uncle Dex was forgetful enough to leave his store unlocked, that was his problem. My conscience got the better of me, though, so I texted him.

Oh man! Uncle Dex texted back. *Not again. Okay, stay there. Be right down.*

So I stayed. Greg, on the other hand, couldn't. "I'll get in trouble with my dad if I'm not home by six-thirty," he said. I knew he wasn't kidding about getting in trouble. His dad was always grounding him — and for stuff you wouldn't think a parent would even notice, like Greg forgetting to put the top back on the toothpaste tube. I felt bad for him.

"I guess I'll see you tomorrow, then," I said.

Greg nodded. I could tell he felt guilty that he couldn't wait with me. And then he brightened a little. "Hey, at least we have our practice space!"

"Yeah," I said, and then we did this complicated secret handshake we made up, and he took off, pedaling furiously to make it home in time.

I went back inside the store to wait for Uncle Dex.

I realized I'd left my beanie down in the basement, so figured I might as well go back down to our new practice room and get it. Plus, I should probably check on where we could plug in our amps.

But when I got down there, the old locker was glowing again, with that same shimmering golden light. I was sure of it this time.

"Whoa," I muttered to myself.

I crossed the room and felt around the edges for the latch.

"Probably treasure," I said out loud.

The locker practically sprung open on its own, but there wasn't any gold inside. No jewelry, no secret stash of money. Just a bunch of old stuff that looked like it was from the military or something: a U.S. Navy peacoat, some sort of army belt buckle, a pair of black boots, a trenching tool, an old army medic's kit, and some other stuff. Nothing that looked too cool.

A draft blew through the room and I started shivering. I hadn't brought a jacket, so I pulled out the peacoat and put it on. It was kind of big on me but really warm — and just like that, the chill was gone.

The glow was gone from the chest, too. I shook my head and looked again. Still no golden glow. I looked around nervously, to make sure I was still alone. The room seemed smaller, more claustrophobic, but probably that was just the shadows. The only light in there was a single naked bulb hanging from the ceiling with a silver chain to turn it off and on. I shut the top of the wooden locker — I'd had enough of that musty smell for one night — and latched it back shut.

I kept the peacoat, though. It was kind of cool, and obviously nobody would ever miss it.

No sooner had I turned to leave, to head back upstairs and wait for Uncle Dex, when I heard something. A voice that sounded so real it made me freeze in my tracks.

The voice said, "That's mine."

I whirled around to see who'd spoken, but nobody was there.

Heart thumping, I ran up the stairs as fast as I could go — so fast that when I got to the front of the store I crashed right into Uncle Dex.

"There's somebody down there!" I yelled.

"In the basement?" Uncle Dex asked.

"Yes! Yes! I heard him!" I kept yelling.

Uncle Dex reached behind the counter and grabbed a baseball bat. "Did you see anybody?"

"Uh, no," I confessed. "Not exactly."

Uncle Dex looked at me hard. "What do you mean, 'Not exactly'?"

"Well, no. I mean, I didn't see anybody. But I did hear somebody. Or something. I mean, I think I did."

I could tell by the look on his face that Uncle Dex was officially skeptical. He dropped the end of the bat on the floor and leaned on the handle.

"Should we go take a look?" he asked.

I thought about the wooden trunk, and the golden glow, and the feeling like I was being watched down there, and the sudden chill, and the peacoat, which I still had on, and the voice that I'd heard, or thought I'd heard. Maybe I was still spooked from Greg scaring me earlier.

"I don't know," I said, sounding pretty lame even to myself. "I might have just gotten nervous or something, being down there alone. It's spooky."

Uncle Dex laughed. "You'll get used to it," he said. "It's not so bad."

I shivered, remembering that voice. Not so bad? I wasn't so sure.

I thought that would be the end of it, but it wasn't. Uncle Dex locked up the store good and tight, and he gave me a ride home, throwing my bike in his trunk even though the lid wouldn't close. But the strangest night of my life had only just begun.

CHAPTER 3

Mom wasn't feeling well when I got home — that happens a lot because of her MS — so I made her some soup and brought it into the bedroom. MS is multiple sclerosis, this disease that messes up your nervous system so sometimes you can't even walk or use your hands, and it makes you supersensitive to all kinds of things, like hot and cold temperatures. There isn't a cure, and it gets worse the longer you have it, with a lot of pain and weakness in your muscles and all. Mom says it comes and goes, and she says her MS isn't as bad as a lot of other people's, but I'm not always so sure about that.

Meanwhile, Dad was stuck in traffic coming home from

Washington, DC, which is something that happens a lot because of his job, and because traffic on Interstate 95 is the worst in America. At least according to my dad.

"Did you have a good day?" Mom asked when I laid the tray next to her on the bed. She looked pale. I'd also made her some hot tea, and I handed her that first.

"Pretty good," I said. "Uncle Dex is going to let me and Greg have our band practice in one of the basement rooms at the shop. We had to clean it all out first, though."

"That's nice," Mom said, taking a sip of tea. "Your uncle Dex could stand to see a friendly face every now and then. Ever since Pop Pop died he's been pretty lonely." Pop Pop was Mom and Uncle Dex's dad.

I missed him, too, of course — he took care of me a lot when I was little and Mom's MS got pretty bad for a while, plus, he was the one who got me interested in history — but I had other things on my mind right at the moment.

"Hey, Mom," I said. "Here's kind of a weird question for you, but I was wondering what your thoughts might be on the subject of ghosts?"

Mom put the teacup back on the saucer and frowned. "Honey, you know Pop Pop is gone, and he's not coming back, no matter how much we miss him, right?"

"I didn't mean Pop Pop," I reassured her. "Just, like, a spirit or something. Like, hypothetically, what if there was a ghost or whatever that might not want you wearing a jacket that belonged to him, and might even say something to you about it, even though you didn't know the jacket was his, and even though you couldn't actually see who was saying it, so you weren't even sure there was anybody saying anything about the jacket in the first place." The words just tumbled out of my mouth. I guess I was still pretty freaked out.

Mom stuck the teacup and saucer onto the tray, sloshing some over the side. "What in heaven's name are you talking about, Anderson?" she asked.

I realized how idiotic I probably sounded. "Nothing. Never mind. It was just something I read about in school. Just something from a book. Forget it. Here, you better eat your soup before it gets cold. You want some crackers? I'll go get you some crackers."

I left as quickly as I could, feeling dumb and embarrassed, before Mom could ask me anything else. Fortunately, Dad came home then, so Mom got distracted talking to him, probably telling him about how strange I was acting. I went into the kitchen to make a sandwich for dinner, since that was about the only meal I knew how to fix besides soup. I made one for Dad, too, and left it on the counter.

"Going to get started on my homework!" I yelled, grabbing my sandwich and a glass of milk. I ducked down the hall and into my bedroom, kicking the door shut behind me.

Right away I noticed something wasn't quite right. I'd tossed the U.S. Navy peacoat on my bed when I first came home, but now it wasn't there. The hair on my neck stood up, and I got goose bumps all over. I tried to convince myself that maybe Dad had done something with it when he got home. But Dad never comes in my room and picks up after me.

I shoved a bunch of papers off my desk and set my sandwich and milk down, then flopped on the bed.

What had I been thinking, asking Mom about ghosts and stuff? *Of course* there were no such things as ghosts.

But there *was* somebody in my room!

I yelped when I saw him, and sat straight up, practically flying off the bed. He was leaning against my bedroom door, holding the navy peacoat.

The intruder glanced up and nodded, but didn't say anything. He quickly went back to examining the peacoat, as if it was the most natural thing in the world. My heart, meanwhile, was practically pounding through my chest. My mind raced through all the possibilities for why a strange guy might be standing in my bedroom, none of them good. Including the possibility that he might belong to the voice I heard in Uncle Dex's basement, and he had followed me home. Did he think I stole his coat? Was he here to get his revenge?

I wanted to yell for Dad, but I was too scared.

The intruder pulled something out of the peacoat pocket — an envelope — and studied it for a minute, then he looked up. I could tell he was just about to say something, but he didn't get the chance because somebody knocked on the bedroom door and opened it. Light from the hallway flooded the room as Dad stepped inside.

"Hey, sport," he said. "Just checking to see how it's going with the homework."

The second Dad opened the door, the intruder suddenly, totally, completely, mysteriously vanished!

Actually, he didn't vanish altogether. This time he left behind the peacoat. And the letter. And me, stammering and stuttering and trying to tell Dad what had just happened, and making no sense at all, even to myself.

Dad finally cut me off and laid his hand on my forehead and said I felt "feverish."

"I'm going to get the thermometer," he said. "There must be something going around. Tonight's an early night for you. Pajamas and bed."

"But, Dad!" I yelled.

"But nothing," he said. "Just calm down and let's get you some rest."

I started to follow him to the hall pantry, since the last thing I wanted was to be alone, but Dad repeated his pajamas-and-bed order. I skipped the pajamas and curled up in a ball under the covers even though I still had my clothes on. Had opening the trunk released some sort of horrible curse?

"There's no such thing as ghosts," I whispered. "There's no such thing as ghosts. There's no such thing as ghosts."

But apparently there *were* such things as ghosts, or whatever the intruder was, because as soon as Dad left the room, he was back. I swallowed hard. Maybe if I stayed under the covers, he'd just take his coat and go. Just thinking that made me feel like a giant baby.

But the ghost didn't seem to notice me. He was just standing there checking out the posters on my wall: a soccer player from Brazil in the World Cup doing a bicycle kick for a goal; Shaun White snowboarding; Mount Everest under a full moon; and, finally, King Kong on top of the Empire

State Building, from the original black-and-white movie they made about a million years ago.

He looked at that one the longest.

Finally, he spoke, but it wasn't at all what I expected. "Hey," he sort of whispered. "I remember that movie." His voice sounded really, really far away, like he was speaking from the other end of a tunnel. There seemed to be an echo to it.

I didn't say anything back. I couldn't speak, and I was afraid I might wet my pants.

"*King Kong*," he said. "I saw it when I was a kid, right when it came out. Once it finally got to our town."

He was dressed in an old-fashioned navy sailor's clothes — white Dixie cup sailor's cap, light blue work shirt, white T-shirt underneath, bell-bottom jeans, black boots — everything scuffed up and tattered and faded. The scariest thing, besides the fact that he was there in the first place, was that he didn't seem to be exactly solid, as if I could see through him to what was on the other side, but not quite. I kept shaking my head hard to clear it out because what I was seeing wasn't possible for me to see. And yet there he was. And there I was, still unable to speak.

"I was a few years younger than you at the time," he said,

still staring at King Kong but talking to me. "You look about twelve. That right?"

I tried to say, "Yes," but only managed to squeak.

He must have understood, though, because he turned to me and smiled a crooked smile. For the first time, I saw his face clearly and could see how young he was — not much more than a teenager. He even had freckles. How could he possibly have seen *King Kong* when it first came out? I was pretty sure that was before my parents were born, probably even before when Pop Pop was a kid.

He kept that crooked smile going and ducked his head as if apologizing for something, then sat down on the end of my bed. The mattress didn't seem to sag underneath him like it always does for anyone else.

I inched as far away as I could, and wondered what had happened to Dad. How long could it possibly take to find a stupid thermometer?

The ghost seemed to be waiting for me to say something, so I tried speaking again and somehow managed a couple of questions: "Who are you?" Quickly followed by "How did you get in here?" and "Please don't hurt me."

He waved his hand, as if brushing away the idea. "Never hurt anybody before, I don't think," he said. "Not directly, anyway. Doubt I'll be starting now. Specially given the circumstances and all."

"The circumstances?" I was back to squeaking.

He started to hand me the letter he'd found in the peacoat and say something else, but then stopped as my bedroom door swung open again. He vanished, leaving behind the coat and the letter, lying on the end of my bed.

Dad was back.

CHAPTER 4

I babbled some more to Dad, trying to tell him what had just happened, but I knew from the worried look on his face that I wasn't making any sense. I kept trying, though, until I even started to doubt what I was saying myself.

Dad eventually got me to stop so he could take my temperature, which was normal, and then he made me take a couple of Extra Strength Something or Other, which must have been pretty powerful because I finally passed out after about an hour. My mind was spinning too fast for me to stay asleep, though, since I woke up again in the middle of the night. I lay there for a long time until I finally got up enough nerve to peek out from under the covers.

There was nobody in my bedroom. I sat up and rubbed my eyes.

The room was bathed in a yellow light that seemed to be coming from outside. Everything still felt spooky, though. And I had that feeling again that I was being watched.

"There's no such things as ghosts." I kept repeating it to myself. "There's no such things as ghosts."

There *were* such things as WWII navy peacoats and old letters, though, and they were both lying on the floor now where I must have kicked them off, next to my bed. I reached over to pick them up, then tossed the coat over the back of my desk chair. The letter was stiff and yellow with age, so dry and brittle I was afraid it might crumble in my hands.

I squinted at the cursive writing. It was addressed to a Miss Betty Corbett in a town in North Carolina I'd never heard of. The return address was too smudged to read. It didn't have a stamp on it, though, so it must not have ever been mailed.

"Hunh," I said to myself.

Somebody cleared his throat on the other side of the room, and this time I jumped up so fast I lost my balance and fell off the bed.

"You okay there?" the now-familiar voice asked, still sounding far, far away, with that faint hint of an echo.

The ghost was back yet again.

"Sorry to scare you," he said as I picked myself up, trembling so hard I couldn't speak. He had already moved to the end of my bed, holding the peacoat and the old letter, which I'd dropped when I fell.

"I might have written this to Betty," he said, waving the letter while I stood there trembling. "It just came to me. Betty was my girl. Way back before everything that happened."

He looked up once again, as if expecting me to say something, but I was too busy forcing myself to take deep breaths and try to calm down — or at least stop freaking out. I slowly eased myself down on the bed, as far away from the ghost as I could without falling off again.

He kept his eyes on me the whole time, with that expectant look on his face, so I took one more deep breath and forced out a response.

"Before what happened?"

He shrugged. "I don't know. But maybe Betty does."

"Is it important? What happened, I mean," I managed to squeak. My hands were shaking. I squeezed them together to make them stop.

He gestured at his faded work uniform. "I think so," he said. "I mean, I'm here, but I don't know how . . ."

He trailed off and got this sad look in his eyes. "I guess I'll just come right out and tell you," he said, "but I don't want you to get all nervous again, okay?"

"Okay," I lied.

He nodded and then continued, "About all I know for sure is there was a war against the Japanese and the Germans, and I was on a ship. Besides that — I mean, how I came to be here — that's what I came to ask your help figuring out. Seems like I've been wandering a long time, not sure where I was, just sort of frustrated and restless. In a kind of, well, limbo is I guess what you'd call it — between where I used to be and where I'm supposed to be going. Then you found my coat and put it on, and that brought me to that room that you and your buddy were cleaning out. And now it brought me here. At least I think that's what happened."

"Wait," I blurted out. A war against the Germans and Japanese? There was only one war that could possibly be . . . "You're saying you were alive during World War II? And just wandering around for over seventy years?" This was all too much for me to take in.

He blinked a couple of times, as if it was his turn to be shocked. "That how long it's been?"

I nodded. "I mean, I guess so," I said, because, of course, this was all impossible: his story, his being here, me sitting on my bed having a conversation with the ghost of a sailor who looked like and said he was from the 1940s!

"Well, anyway," he said. "Something pulled me back here for a reason, and that reason must be you, to help me figure out where I need to go and what I need to do. Starting with finding Betty."

He waved the letter again. "I must have written her this," he said. "So I'm betting we can find out all kinds of things once she opens it."

"Like what?" I asked

"Like what I go by, for starters, and then what I was doing in the war, and how I came to be missing."

I sat up straighter. "You don't know your own name?"

The ghost frowned and furrowed his brow, struggling to remember. Then he exhaled hard and shook his head.

"What about dog tags?" I asked. "Aren't soldiers — and sailors — supposed to wear their dog tags around their necks on a chain, with their name and stuff, in case something happens to them?" I was pretty sure that's what Pop Pop had told me.

The ghost patted the front of his shirt and then shook his head again. "Must have lost mine."

I suggested we just open the letter and see what it said for ourselves, but he didn't like that idea.

"It isn't right to open other people's mail," the ghost said. "Plus, it's against the law. Or it used to be."

"But you wrote it," I pointed out.

"True," he said. "Least I think so. Can't be too sure about that, either. Guess we can ask Betty. Once we find her."

"What?" I said. "No. I mean, I don't think I can do that. I have school. I wouldn't know where to begin. I wouldn't know how." Even as I was saying the words, there was this tiny part of me — I guess it was the history-nut part that I got from Pop Pop — that actually, kind of, sort of liked the idea of maybe helping solve the mystery of what happened to a ghost from World War II.

He didn't say anything, just laid the letter back down on the bed. The peacoat, too.

"Don't you want to keep those?" I asked, worried that he would leave them with me and have an excuse to come back.

"You might change your mind about reading the letter," I added. "And you might get cold."

The ghost shook his head. "I don't exactly get cold," he said. "Hot, either."

He stood up from the bed. "It's late and you're just a boy," he continued. "So I'm going to go now and let you get some sleep. And so you can think things over."

He looked straight in my eyes and held his gaze there.

"I need your help," he said in that faraway voice. "I have a feeling that this might be the only chance I get to find out what happened to me."

He paused. "And so maybe I can finally get some rest."

When I blinked, he went from semisolid to translucent, and then from translucent to transparent.

When I blinked again, he went from transparent to invisible, though his voice lingered a little while longer.

"See you tomorrow, Anderson."

That took all the air out of me. This guy didn't know his own name, but somehow he knew mine.

CHAPTER 5

HOW I ever got back to sleep was a giant mystery, but somehow I did. Dad must have yelled up to me twenty times in the morning to get up, it was time for school, but I just kept pressing my pillow down hard over my head until he came in, turned on the light, pulled the covers off my bed, and left me lying there shivering — partly from being cold and partly from still being scared of the ghost.

Dad was gone to work by the time I finally dragged myself downstairs. Mom was having a hard morning with her MS, so I decided I shouldn't bother her about what happened last night. Or about what I *dreamed* happened last night, which is what I tried to convince myself it must have been. Without really thinking about it, I pulled on the pea-coat and tucked the letter to Miss Betty Corbett in my backpack as I ran outside to try to catch the bus.

It was already pulling away, though, so I had to walk. That's the kind of day it turned out to be.

I was so late for school that I didn't get a chance to talk to Greg. We didn't have any classes together in the morning. Julie Kobayashi was in my math class, though, and I was pretty sure she smiled at me, or as close to a smile as I'd ever seen from her. More like the absence of her usual frown, along with what appeared to be a nod of her head when our eyes met briefly.

She also sat down next to me at lunch, something else that had never happened before.

"We should get started right away," she said.

This caught me by surprise. "Get started with what?" I asked.

"Band practice," she said. "Greg told me you changed your mind about having me in the band. I don't know why you didn't say yes in the first place. I'm very good on the keyboards. But thank you."

Before I could say anything back, she laid several sheets of paper next to my lunch tray. Music and lyrics. "I wrote some of these," she said. "The others are contemporary songs. And some classic songs that I learned from my dad. I figured we could start with these. I printed out copies for both of you during study hall this morning. Also for your uncle."

"Wait," I said, bewildered. "My uncle?"

"Yes." She nodded. "Electric ukulele, correct?"

"Well, sort of," I said. "But, I mean, did you and Greg come up with all this?" I waved at the sheet music. "These songs and everything?"

She frowned. "Of course. I explained what our band should play. He understood. He did say that perhaps I should write out chords and draw pictures to show the proper fingering for guitar." She pointed to the music. "As you can see, I did that as well."

Julie stood up. "I'm going to get my lunch now. I'll bring my keyboard to your uncle's store this afternoon after school."

I nodded and said okay, all the while thinking I was pretty sure I was going to have to kill Greg.

He showed up a few minutes after Julie left, and I let him have it. "What the heck, Greg! Julie Kobayashi? Really?"

He grinned. "Yeah. Saw her this morning before school. So no need to worry about your uncle on keyboards. Although I did mention that he might be sitting in sometimes on his uke. You're welcome."

"We never decided about this," I said.

Greg scrunched his face, a sign that he was thinking really hard. "We didn't? Are you sure? I mean, you said you didn't want Uncle Dex in the band and all. I just figured, you know, that meant Julie was in."

He paused. Then continued, "Anyway, I kind of think she likes me."

I grabbed his sleeve. "Are you serious? This is Julie Kobayashi we're talking about. She doesn't like anybody."

Greg pulled himself loose and smoothed out his sleeve. "Well, she smiled at me," he said.

I didn't believe him. "Really? Like an actual smile?"

"Yes," he said firmly. "Really. Anyway, I already told her she's in the band, so she's in the band. Boy, are you a total grouch today." He stood up with his tray, though he hadn't eaten anything yet. Neither of us had. "See you this afternoon."

He had Julie's sheet music stuffed into the back pocket of his jeans. I saw it as he walked away to the other side of the lunchroom — to sit with Julie, as it turned out.

"Well, this is just *great*," I said to myself.

"What is?" a familiar voice asked.

I did a double take like you see in the movies, but I guess I was too tired and too irritated by everything to react much more than that, even though the ghost was suddenly sitting right next to me.

"How did you get in here?" I asked.

He shrugged. "Can't exactly say." He looked around the cafeteria. "This place looks kind of familiar."

"If you've seen one school cafeteria, you've smelled them all," I said, as if I was talking to just anybody. And then I got nervous. "Can anybody else see you, besides me?" I asked, worried that I would get into trouble. Or worse, that there would be a scene, with security guards and police and me in the middle of it, and then I would be marked forever, or at least for all of middle school, as that weird kid hanging out at lunch with some guy — some *ghost*! — in a sailor suit.

"*You* can," he said. "Can't say about your friends. Maybe the girl."

And sure enough, Julie Kobayashi had stopped chewing in midbite and was staring across the room at us.

I didn't even bother to pick up my lunch tray. I just bolted out of the cafeteria, down the hall, and into the bathroom.

It didn't matter. The ghost somehow ended up there, too, leaning against a sink.

"Didn't mean to upset you," he said. "Just wondering if you'd thought over what we talked about last night." He pointed to my backpack, which wouldn't fit in my locker so I carried it with me all day. "I see you brought the letter with you."

"How can you tell?" I asked. "It's *inside*!"

He shrugged again. "Some things you just know."

"Okay, look," I said, desperate to make him go away. "How about if I mail it for you? I'll get a stamp. I'll take it down to the post office right after school."

The ghost just looked at me.

Of course that was a stupid thing to suggest. "You're right," I said, though he hadn't spoken. "They might not be able to deliver it. She might not live at that address any-more. And I guess we wouldn't exactly be able to talk to her, either, and find out, you know, your name and all."

Somebody came in the bathroom. A kid in my grade named Grady Ornish.

"Hey, Grady," I said, hoping he wouldn't notice the navy guy/ghost/whatever standing right next to me. Apparently he didn't, probably because the ghost had already disappeared, though I could tell somehow that he was still there in the restroom.

"Hey, Anderson," Grady said. "What's going on?"

"Oh, you know," I said. "The usual."

The now-invisible ghost chuckled when I said that. "The usual." As if. I almost had to laugh, too.

"What was that sound?" Grady asked. "Did you hear something?"

I shook my head and said, "Probably just the toilets."

CHAPTER 6

I tried looking Miss Betty Corbett up on the Internet, at the address on the envelope, in that North Carolina town, but got nothing.

I tried every search engine I could think of, but still came up with a big, fat zero, unless Betty Corbett was twenty-seven years old and had been convicted of murder last year in South Dakota. Or she was a fifty-five-year-old advice columnist. Or an eleven-year-old flute player with her own YouTube channel.

I asked Mom that afternoon after school how to find out what happened to somebody from a long time ago.

"How long?" she asked. She'd just come back from physical therapy and was pretty wiped out, sitting back in Dad's recliner in the living room, holding an ice pack. It was for her hands, which she said felt as if they were on fire a lot of the time (it had something to do with her MS).

"Like about seventy years," I said.

"And what is this all about?" she asked.

I figured there wasn't any harm in telling her about the letter I'd found in the navy peacoat at Uncle Dex's store, though I left out the part about the ghost.

"Why not just open it?" Mom asked after I explained. "After all this time, it's likely that the person isn't even alive anymore."

"But they could be," I said, showing her the envelope. "Anyway, I thought maybe if I could track this lady down, and maybe write about it, I could get some extra credit or something in school."

Mom laid her ice pack down and dried her hands, then took the letter. "You could call the courthouse down there in North Carolina, I suppose," she said. "Ask if this Betty Corbett is listed anywhere in their property records, or if she ever got a marriage license and changed her name. Or if there's a death certificate. That sort of thing."

"Do you think I could text them instead?" I asked hopefully.

Mom smiled but shook her head. "No. Sorry. You're going to have to man up on this one, Anderson."

I sighed and retrieved the envelope and left.

The ghost was waiting for me in my bedroom.

"What does that mean — 'man up'?" he asked.

I explained as I gathered up my guitar and amplifier and Julie Kobayashi's sheet music.

"Gotta go to band practice," I said when I finished, but when I looked up, he had already vanished.

· · ·

It was hard riding my bike with everything balanced on the handlebars, so it took me a while to get downtown to the Kitchen Sink.

"Hey, rock and roller," Uncle Dex said when I walked in. I didn't actually see him when he said this because he was totally hidden behind a giant pile of used books somebody had left on the counter. How he knew it was me was another great mystery of the day.

"Hey, Uncle Dex," I said. "Anybody else here yet?"

"Not anybody," he said back. "*Every*body. Though I haven't heard them start actually practicing yet. Afraid I'm too busy this afternoon to join you guys on my ukulele."

"Maybe next time," I said to be polite, and dragged my guitar and amp down the narrow stairs to the basement. I had been so excited when Greg and I came up with the idea of the band, and when Uncle Dex said we could practice down in his basement and everything. Now, though, I felt the weight of the world on me. This ghost business. Julie Kobayashi joining the band. Having to talk on the phone to some strangers in North Carolina about a lady nobody probably even knew.

"Anderson!" Greg shouted when he saw me in the door. "Check this out!" He swung his arm dramatically behind him to reveal none other than the ghost, who had obviously beaten me there.

The ghost waved, and I gave a faint wave back.

"So you guys met, huh?" I asked.

"Oh yeah," Greg said. "We met all right. You should have been here half an hour ago for the totally flipping out part. I thought I was going to faint when he showed up like that — you know, just all of a sudden sort of materializing here and everything."

"Sorry again about scaring you," the ghost said to Greg. He was leaning against the wall, though he didn't seem to be disturbing the dust.

Julie Kobayashi crossed her arms over her chest. "He didn't frighten me," she said. "Only Greg. I had already seen him before. Back at the cafeteria." She paused. "Actually, not him as he is now. More the *idea* of him."

"But he explained already," Greg said, surprisingly calm for a guy who had just met a ghost. It kind of made me annoyed. It had taken me all night long, and then some, but Greg — and Julie — seemed to have adjusted just fine, and in what I was betting to be record time.

Julie ran her hands over her keyboard, though it wasn't turned on yet. "We have agreed to help." She looked at the ghost and nodded again. He nodded back.

I sat down on my amplifier. "I have to make some phone calls to try to find this lady he's looking for," I said. "But can we please have band practice first?"

Everybody thought that was a good idea, including the ghost, who had found a beat-up old trumpet somewhere in the bowels of the Kitchen Sink. Greg and I tuned our guitars as best we could to Julie's keyboard, and then we stumbled through the first song in the pile of music she had decided we should play. We sounded terrible, which wasn't surprising. When the ghost tried to come in on his horn, though, it got *really* terrible.

We all stopped playing at once. The ghost blinked at us, looked down at the trumpet, then back at us again. "I remembered I used to play. At least I think I did. High school band, maybe?"

"Are you *sure* about that?" Greg asked.

Julie, who was all business, suggested he go off into another room and work on his "skills." I'm not sure if that hurt his feelings, but he did that fade-out thing again that I'd seen a couple of times. I wasn't sure how all this ghost stuff worked yet. The horn went with him, and that was fine with us.

"Wow," Greg said. "That was the worst."

Our second time through wasn't much better than before, but I was pretty sure there was at least a little bit of improvement. Julie must have thought so, too, because her deep frown lifted to medium, so that was a little bit of improvement.

We hammered through a couple of more songs over the next hour and then decided that was enough for our first day. "Don't want to burn out or anything," Greg said. Julie didn't disagree, which for her probably amounted to the same thing.

"Hey," Greg said, remembering. "What about a name for our band? We have to have a name."

"Any ideas?" I asked.

Julie furrowed her brow, obviously thinking very seriously about the question of band names.

Greg brightened. "How about something to do with your, uh, friend?" We couldn't hear the ghost practicing down the hall, if he was even still around, but it was impossible to forget about him, of course.

Greg and I threw out a bunch of different names — the Sailors, the Graveyarders, the Invisibles — but Julie said no to all of them. She didn't explain, but she probably didn't need to.

"Well, what do you suggest?" I asked Julie. "You don't like anybody else's ideas."

She furrowed her brow even further, and went into her deepest frown yet. Her black bangs practically covered her eyes. She stayed like that until I thought she'd frozen, and then her face lifted.

She leaned in close to us, as if sharing some great secret, and whispered, "We'll be the Ghosts of War."

• • • •

The ghost didn't follow me home, and he didn't show up when I got there. Even after dinner, when I went to my room to do homework, he never showed up. I was still trying to figure out how this ghost stuff worked exactly: where he could be and when he could be there; who could see him and talk to him; where he went when he disappeared; whether he had any superpowers.

Just before I went to bed, my phone rang and it was Greg, totally freaking out about the ghost.

"Delayed reaction?" I asked.

"You have no idea," he gasped.

I said I thought I probably did and then spent the next half hour listening to him stammering and babbling until he finally wore himself out and said he was going to bed.

I was a little surprised, but not as much as I thought, when I got a text a few minutes later from Julie Kobayashi, who I guessed was also freaking out, but in her own quiet way.

She said she was just checking to see if I was okay.

I said I was, and asked if she was having a delayed reaction to the ghost, like Greg.

Of course not, she texted me back, which, of course, I took to mean "Of course."

CHAPTER 7

During study hall the next day at school, I braced myself, got a hall pass to go to the bathroom, and sat on a toilet to call Dooley, North Carolina, the town where Betty Corbett lived, or at least where she lived when the ghost wrote the letter. I'd gotten the number from the Internet.

I was pretty happy at first because it seemed like nobody was going to pick up. I was also surprised that it didn't ring to voice mail, or even just go to one of those automatic answering services right away, where they tell you to press one for this and two for that, and by the time they get to nine you've forgotten what most of the options were and so you just hang up and decide you didn't need to make that call anyway.

"Hello," a lady's voice said. "Dooley Courthouse. How may I direct your call?"

I'd written out my questions on a sheet of folded-up paper and nearly dropped my phone as I fumbled it open, which I should have already done. I was balancing a lot on my lap while perched on the toilet — my backpack, my notebook, my pencil, the list of questions.

"I am calling to request information on someone," I read.

"Okay," the lady said. "Fire away, honey."

I wasn't expecting the "Fire away, honey," and it threw me for a second. But then I kept going.

"Her name is Betty Corbett," I continued reading, "and I am hoping that you have a telephone number or address or marriage license or death certificate or some way to get in touch with her."

The lady at the Dooley, North Carolina, courthouse was quiet for a minute, and then she asked me, "Who is this?"

"This is — I mean, I'm, just, I mean I just have something I'm trying to get to her. It's this old letter that I found," I said in a rush, not really prepared for her question.

"Where you calling from?" she asked.

"Um, Virginia."

"And your name again?"

"Anderson Carter," I replied, wondering if I was going to be in trouble.

"And just how old are you, Anderson Carter?"

I told her I was twelve, and then I told her I was calling from my school. About the only thing I left out was that I was sitting on a toilet.

"And you found a letter for her?" the lady asked. "Who is it from, and why didn't you just put it in the mail? And what's it doing up in Virginia?"

I said it was hard to explain totally, but that I found it in a junk shop my uncle owned and that my grandfather used to own before he died and it was so old I didn't think she still lived at the address on it — and there I went babbling again, with all this stuff she didn't need to know and I didn't know why I was telling her, though I did remember to tell her the address on the letter and that I couldn't read the return address, so I didn't know who it was from.

"Do you know who I am?" the lady asked.

This stumped me. Of course I didn't know who she was. "No," I said.

"I'm her granddaughter," the lady said. "Arlene DeMille. Betty Corbett is my grandmother. Only that's not her name. Hasn't been since she married my grandfather. She's Betty DeMille. And I'm pretty sure that address was where she used to live when she was a girl, before she married my granddaddy, Glenn DeMille."

"So you said she *is* your grandmother? So she's still, you know, *alive*?"

Arlene laughed. "She sure is, honey. She's in her nineties, but she still goes for her walks every day."

"And her name is Betty DeMille now?" I asked, just to be sure. "I mean, like, Mrs. Glenn DeMille?"

Arlene laughed. "That's right."

I felt a strange sort of breeze just then, even though I was still hiding in a stall and the bathroom window was closed. I looked up, half expecting the ghost to be there. He wasn't, at least not that I could see.

Arlene said it was awfully sweet of me to get in touch about the letter and that she was really curious to know who it was from.

"How about I give you her current address," Arlene said. "Maybe you can put it in a bigger envelope for safety and mail it on down here. I know she'll get a kick out of getting something from back whenever. And you say there's no return address? No name on there for whoever wrote this letter?"

"No," I said. "He didn't put his name on it."

"He?" She sounded surprised. "He who?"

I wasn't about to mention the ghost, so I said, "Oh, I just meant whoever it was, you know. I mean, it's not a bill or anything. They wrote it by hand and all. It's very good hand-writing. But it does look like the way a guy would write, I think. Maybe." There I was, babbling again.

I swallowed hard and then asked, "Do you think it'd be all right if my friends and I delivered the letter?" I figured I could convince Uncle Dex to drive.

"I think my grandma would like that very much," she said, sounding surprised.

I thought she'd ask more questions, but the bell rang just then and so I thanked her and said I had to go to my next class.

I didn't get all the way out of the bathroom, though, because the ghost was standing right outside the stall. I nearly ran into him — if that was possible.

He had the strangest look on his face.

"What?" I asked when I got over being startled and got my breath back.

"Glenn DeMille," he said.

"Okay?"

"I think I know that name."

"That's great," I said, grinning. "But I kind of have to get to class right now, so maybe we can talk about it later."

The ghost didn't step out of the way, and I wasn't about to see if I could just walk through him.

He looked at me, straight in the eyes, with that strange look still on his face. And then he said, "I think he might have been my best friend."

$$\bullet \quad \bullet \quad \bullet$$

It was four hours to Dooley, North Carolina. The only way we could convince Uncle Dex to drive was to tell him about the letter, the same as with Mom — but, of course, not about the ghost. Obviously, there was nothing Uncle Dex liked more than a historical mystery. Every piece of junk that came into his shop, he insisted on knowing the story behind it — who used to own it, where they lived, what happened to them, why the person was getting rid of whatever it was: rocking chair, picture frame, Confederate money, signed copy of *The Phantom Tollbooth*.

The ghost sat in the back of the van. Or he sort of sat there, anyway. He'd barely spoken to me, to any of us, since my conversation with Arlene DeMille. And now, sitting back there alone in Uncle Dex's Econoline van, he kept flickering in and out of view. At least I guessed that was what was going on back there. The rest of us were pretty quiet, too — "unnerved" was probably the right word for how we felt.

Uncle Dex, on the other hand, babbled just about the whole time as he drove, and kept putting on different old songs, telling us we should do some songs by this band or that band, or "Never mind about these guys," or "Whoa, didn't remember how bad those dorks were."

Somewhere south of Richmond, Greg asked Julie about her mom and dad, and that led to all of us talking about our families.

Julie's Mom was American. Her dad was Japanese. "Everybody thinks my mom must have been a hippie," she said. "One of those girls who graduates college and goes to Japan and teaches English and marries the serious Japanese man. But it was the opposite. My dad was the one with the guitar, always just wanting to play his music. When my mom visited Japan, she was on a business trip, but they met and fell in love anyway.

"I'm like my mom in my manner," she added, sounding very formal. "I'm like my dad in my clothes and music." She didn't explain beyond that.

Greg told Julie about his mom and dad when she finished: "They're divorced. I mostly live with my dad."

What he didn't mention was that his dad was older — old enough to be his grandfather — and his mother had moved to another state and only saw Greg for one month during the summer and every other Christmas. They talked on the phone sometimes, too, but not all that much.

"Anderson's dad is a spy," he said, quickly changing the subject. "Works in DC."

"No he's not," I corrected Greg. "He just works for the government."

"Doing what?" Julie asked.

"I don't really know," I said with a shrug. "He's not allowed to talk about it."

"Oh," she said. "So he *is* a spy."

"No," I said, though the truth was I'd always wished that was the case, but I'd never known one way or another. Dad wouldn't talk about it. Whenever I brought it up, he just said the same thing: He worked for the government and it wasn't very interesting. End of story.

The conversation died there, and I turned my attention to the real mystery sitting in the far back of the van. I was worried about the ghost ever since we found out Betty had probably married his best friend, Glenn DeMille. He just seemed so sad after we heard that, though he didn't say anything more about it — except that he needed to go down there, and the letter still had to be delivered.

I turned around to check on him, but the ghost flickered out just as I did. Greg and Julie saw it, too, and they both shivered. I must have shivered, too, because Uncle Dex asked if we were cold, and did we want him to roll up his window.

CHAPTER 8

Arlene DeMille met us at the Dooley Retirement Home, which wasn't hard to find, even though Uncle Dex didn't have a GPS. He said he preferred a good, old-fashioned map. Apparently, the town of Dooley, North Carolina, hadn't changed much since the 1980s, which was when Uncle Dex's map was published.

It was a pretty tiny town, with a lot of trees, surrounded by rolling hills and acres and acres of peanut fields, hog farms, and tobacco crops.

"Welcome," Arlene said before we all even piled out of Uncle Dex's van. We introduced ourselves all around and then she turned to me.

"Grandma Betty is just beside herself about the letter," she said. "I already explained about how you found it in your uncle's junk shop."

"Antique store," Uncle Dex corrected her. " 'Curio shop' is okay, too."

Arlene just smiled.

Five minutes later, we were standing outside the door to Betty Corbett's room. Arlene said she thought it should just be her and me going in to deliver the letter. "It's a very small room," she explained. "And I don't want her to get overwhelmed by too much company all at once."

So everybody else stayed outside while we went in. Betty — Mrs. DeMille — was asleep in a stuffed recliner next to a window. The window was open and there were half a dozen birds in a bird feeder just outside. Mrs. DeMille had a bag of birdseed in her lap.

She nearly spilled it when Arlene woke her up.

"Grandma Betty," she said softly. "This is the young man I was telling you about. His name is Anderson Carter, and he's from Virginia."

Mrs. DeMille smiled a warm, wrinkly smile. You could tell she was somebody who had always smiled a lot in her life. "All the way from Virginia!" she said. "Well, sit down, sit down." She patted the bed next to her.

"I'm sorry I don't have another chair to offer you," she said. "But I'm afraid there's just no room."

"This is okay," I said as Arlene and I sat on the bed. Then I held out the envelope. "Here's the letter," I said. "I hope it's a good one."

I didn't see the ghost anywhere in the room. I kept glancing around, wondering if he would show up.

Mrs. DeMille didn't mess around once she had the envelope. She picked up a silver letter opener and with one quick, neat slice had it open.

The letter inside was a piece of paper so thin it practically didn't even exist. Mrs. DeMille lifted her glasses, which had been hanging on a string around her neck, up onto her nose. She didn't say much, hardly even breathed as she read.

At one point, she touched her heart and said, "Oh." And then, a little later, "Oh, dear."

And then she started crying. The glasses slipped off her nose and dropped down in front of her. She reached for a tissue.

"What is it, Grandma Betty?" Arlene asked. "Who is it from? What does it say?"

I still didn't see the ghost, although I had a feeling that he was in the room somewhere, just not visible. I felt one of those phantom breezes, like the one in the school bathroom when I hid in the stall to make the call to the Dooley Courthouse. It had to be him.

It took Mrs. DeMille a few minutes to compose herself and speak. "It's from a boy I knew a long, long time ago," she said. "A dear, sweet boy."

"A boy, Grandma Betty?" Arlene encouraged her to continue.

"Yes," Mrs. DeMille said. "He was my first boyfriend. It was before the war, and then the war started and he was determined to go." She started crying again, but kept speaking. "He was just seventeen, but his parents let him enlist early, in the navy. He always loved the ocean. And he was your grandfather's best friend. Those two — they were inseparable. Your granddaddy tried to enlist with him, but his parents wanted him to finish school first, so they didn't let him go."

I hadn't said a word so far, but now I had to ask because I was dying to know: "What was his name?"

Mrs. DeMille smiled a sad smile. "William Foxwell."

Arlene asked her grandmother if she had been in love with this William Foxwell. "I mean, before Grandaddy," she added.

Mrs. DeMille kept that sad smile on her face. "I suppose I was," she said. "I know it broke my heart when we got the news. It broke all of our hearts."

"What news?" I asked.

"Why, that he had died," she said. "Well, actually not that. They said that he was missing in action and *presumed* to be dead. But I don't suppose if you're missing in action in the Pacific Ocean, and they can't find you anywhere on your ship, that there's any chance to survive."

"What ship was he on, Grandma Betty?" she asked.

Mrs. DeMille couldn't remember. "I'm so sorry," she said. "I never knew. It was so long ago, and I hated to think about it so much, about what might have happened to him. I do remember he had some sort of rank, though it wasn't very high. A seaman second-class. Your granddaddy, he was heartbroken, too, of course. It was what you might say brought us together — trying to help each other through all that sadness and grief."

I felt pretty bad for them, listening to Mrs. DeMille, and thinking about the ghost — William Foxwell, or the William Foxwell she knew seventy years ago.

Arlene asked her grandmother what the letter said. Miss Corbett handed it to her. "Oh, you two are welcome to read it. It's as sweet a letter as could be, and I know I must look so sad, and I am, but it has also made me very, very happy."

I looked over Arlene's shoulder so I could see the letter, too, as she read it silently to herself. I was pretty sure, even though I still couldn't see him, that William Foxwell was looking over my shoulder, too.

Hi, Betty —

I hope you're well. I am well, too, or as well as can be expected under the circumstances. However, I can't write much more than that in this letter. Just in case it fell into enemy hands. "Loose lips might sink ships," and all that. Anyway, we're up to something big is all I can tell you. I don't know what's going to happen to me or to any of us but I pray every night for everybody on board.

There's something I've been meaning to tell you, about the first time I ever saw you, back in about the first grade. I knew right then that I wouldn't ever even look at another girl. And I still feel that way, Betty. I really do. But I also know that things can happen to you. I mean, it is a war, and the Japanese mean business and don't I know it from what happened to us back at Coral Sea.

So what this is all leading up to is this: If something happens to me — not that it will, of course, but JUST IN CASE — then I think you could do a whole lot worse than to take up with Glenn DeMille. You probably don't know that he always had a big crush on you, too, but lucky me, I asked you out first and once I did that, he was too good of a friend to say anything. But some things you just kind of figure out as you go along and this is one of them.

Now, if I come through all in one piece, the way I plan to, this letter won't even get mailed. I'm putting it in my coat where somebody will find it and give it to you if I don't come back.

And in the meanwhile every time I see the moon is full, I will think about you, and will likely also do so even when the moon is not full.

Yours forever,

William

I found out a lot more before saying good-bye to Mrs. DeMille. Her husband — William's best friend — passed away a couple of years ago. They had always lived in Dooley and raised all three of their children there. The youngest boy they actually named William, after William Foxwell. He was Arlene's dad.

There didn't seem to be any way to find out more about what happened to the ghost in the war because William Foxwell's family was all gone now and none of his relatives still lived in Dooley. He never had any brothers or sisters.

Mrs. DeMille kept thanking me for finding the letter

and delivering it to her. She said it brought her some peace of mind, to find out that William had wanted her to marry Glenn all along.

"I didn't feel guilty when I started seeing Glenn," she said. "But I did always wonder about how it might make William feel. And now I know."

She said I should keep the navy peacoat, which I'd also brought to give her if she wanted it.

. . .

Of course, Greg and Julie and Uncle Dex wanted to know everything as soon as I stepped out of the room, but we waited until we got out to the van before I told them the whole story about the visit.

There were a lot of "Wows!" and "No ways!" as I recounted the conversation, until Uncle Dex spotted a church yard sale and pulled over to check it out.

William Foxwell showed up in the backseat almost as soon as he left.

He didn't say anything at first, and I figured he was overwhelmed by emotion and all, the way anybody would be, of course. I mean, how often do you get to watch your old girlfriend from seventy years ago read a letter you wrote to her — also seventy years ago — telling her it's okay to marry your best friend if something happens to you in the war?

I'm betting on just about never.

Then William Foxwell started talking. "Glenn and me," he said, "we went out for the football team in high school, but neither one of us made it, which was kind of a surprise because our school was so small we almost didn't have enough guys for a team in the first place. But we got cut anyway, which really stung."

He paused and then continued, not looking at any of us, just sort of staring at nothing. "So we decided our game was baseball, and we started practicing every chance we could get. Betty came out and practiced with us, which a girl just about never did back then, but she didn't care."

Greg, who loved a good story more than anybody, interrupted. "So you guys turned out to be the stars of the baseball team?"

William Foxwell shook his head. "Not exactly. Turned out that even with all that practice only one of us was any good at baseball."

"Was it you?" Greg asked.

"Was it Glenn?" Julie asked.

William Foxwell shook his head again, and smiled. "No. It was Betty."

He didn't say anything else for a while, just sat there, I guess busy remembering these things from when he was young.

"After Mama and Daddy signed to let me enlist," he said, finally, "that's about all I remember up to."

"Not what ship you were on?" Julie asked.

"What about Coral Sea?" I asked. "You said something about Coral Sea in your letter to Betty. Do you remember anything about that?"

William Foxwell seemed to kind of flicker, as though there was some sort of interruption in the signal and we were getting a bad connection.

He started to say something else — I thought it was about Coral Sea, wherever that was — but we couldn't follow what he said. Too much static.

Uncle Dex came back with an armload of junk from the yard sale just then. William Foxwell went silent when Dex pulled open the rear doors to toss it all in the van — still there with us for the rest of the trip home, but not quite.

·   ·   ·

Uncle Dex knew quite a bit about Coral Sea, as it turned out — or rather the Battle of the Coral Sea — which didn't surprise me, knowing what a history nut he was, just like me.

"Oh yeah," he said when I asked, once we were back on the interstate and heading north to Virginia. "Well, you guys know about the Japanese attack on Pearl Harbor in Hawaii, right? The one that destroyed half the U.S. naval fleet on December 7, 1941? President Roosevelt called it 'a date which will live in infamy.'"

Uncle Dex glanced in the rearview mirror back at Julie. "No offense," he added.

Julie didn't say anything.

"Oh yeah," Greg said to Julie. "I almost forgot you were, like, half Japanese."

Julie gave him a withering look. "I am an American."

Greg ducked as if he thought she might hit him. Julie rolled her eyes.

"So," Uncle Dex continued, "as I was saying. A few months after Pearl Harbor, the Imperial Japanese Navy was all ready to invade New Guinea, another island in the Pacific Ocean."

"Why New Guinea?" I asked. "And where is that exactly?"

Julie answered my second question. "It is north of Australia."

"So what happened?" Greg asked, clearly glad the subject was no longer Julie's ethnicity.

Uncle Dex fielded the question. "The Japanese had been kicking the Allies' butt all over the Pacific for months, ever since Pearl Harbor. They already controlled most of the islands in the South Pacific and most of what's called the Pacific Rim — China, Southeast Asia, the Philippines. If they captured New Guinea, they would have been able to isolate Australia, cutting them off from the war effort. And then probably attack Hawaii again. And maybe even the West Coast of the U.S. So we had to stop them.

"At first, the Battle of the Coral Sea was shaping up to be one of those huge naval battles," he continued. "Aircraft carriers, battleships, cruisers, destroyers, submarines — the whole armada thing. Japan versus the U.S. and Australia."

"Wait a minute," Greg interrupted. "What's the difference between all those ships you just listed?"

"I've got this," I said to Uncle Dex. I had read all about World War II ships, and seen a lot of pictures in one of Pop Pop's old books. "The aircraft carriers have big, long, open decks so planes can fly off them and attack their targets, like on land or other ships, and then the planes can come back and land on the aircraft carrier again. But carriers have a hard time defending themselves because they don't have a lot of cannons and antiaircraft weapons and stuff, so they need the cruisers to protect them from anybody trying to attack them. The cruisers have a lot of big guns and stuff, but no planes."

"What about destroyers?" Greg asked.

"You use those to find and try to destroy the submarines," I said. "The submarines are busy trying to sink ships from under the water, using their torpedoes."

It was Julie's turn to ask a question, though I could tell she didn't like not already knowing something. "And battleships?"

Uncle Dex jumped in on this one. "They're designed for invasions from the sea," he said. "They have long-range cannons to pound away at targets miles away, like usually on land. If your battleships can take them out first, then when you land your own troops on the beach for the invasion, they have a better chance of surviving and your invasion has a better chance of succeeding."

Greg shook his head. "Too much to remember," he said.

Uncle Dex and I just smiled.

"Well, anyway," Uncle Dex said, "to get back to the story, the Japanese and American ships never actually fired on one another at Coral Sea. They never got close enough. Instead, they attacked each other's ships with the planes from their aircraft carriers. Both sides had torpedo planes and dive-bombers in the air and there were ships everywhere and it was all very confusing. If I remember right, a bunch of American bombers mistakenly attacked some American ships during the battle, thinking they were bombing the Japanese. Neither side actually won the battle, but I guess you could say the Allies sort of won because the Japanese weren't able to land their invasion forces in New Guinea. Plus, it was a major morale boost for the Allied forces since it was the first time they'd pushed back the Japanese."

Even though I knew a lot about ships, I'd never heard about any of this Coral Sea stuff before — and neither had Greg or Julie. It was cool learning about it, though, especially since it might be taking us one step closer to solving the mystery of William Foxwell. Now we just had to find out which ship he'd been on, and what happened to him and to that particular ship afterward.

I had a hundred questions I wanted to ask William Foxwell besides stuff about the war, like how was he feeling about everything Mrs. DeMille had said. And about meeting her again after all these years — not that they actually got to meet. The last time he'd seen her she would have been really young, like seventeen — the same as him. And now there she was, an old woman.

And his best friend was dead.

I looked at Greg and just watched him for a while, wondering how I'd feel if it was him and me in place of William Foxwell and his friend Glenn DeMille. I couldn't imagine Greg not being here anymore, though, and I bet William and Glenn felt the same way about each other, too.

A part of me actually relaxed on the drive home, figuring we'd pretty much done our job. We knew the ghost's name now, and where he was from, and all about his old girlfriend. We knew he'd been in the war. There were a few more details we still needed to fill in for him, but that was about all. That's what I thought, anyway.

But, boy, was I wrong.

We were just getting started — and if we were going to help William Foxwell, we were going to have to move fast.

CHAPTER 10

I couldn't sleep that night.

No big surprise. So I was awake at midnight when William Foxwell showed up. Once again, one minute he wasn't there, and then the next minute he was. There was still some flickering, but not too much, and this time at least I could follow what he was saying.

"I remembered why I wrote that part about the full moon," he said, as if we'd been in the middle of a conversation, and that was the subject. "I used to drive by Betty's house sometimes at night, hoping I might see her sitting on her porch, maybe, or taking out the trash for the next morning, or coming home from choir practice at her church. It was always the best on a full moon because we didn't have streetlights or anything like that back then in Dooley, and when it was a full moon I could see her a lot better."

"Would you stop and talk to her?" I asked.

William Foxwell shook his head. "Not usually. Not unless she happened to see me. Sometimes she would. She'd yell, 'William Foxwell, what are you doing out so late?' Like she was getting on me about breaking my curfew or something." He laughed. "She'd make me come in and drink some lemonade. Her dad would give me a hard look, but I don't think he meant anything by it. He was just being her dad, doing what dads do."

He paused, then continued, "I figured one day I'd be doing the same thing if Betty and I got married and had kids and some boy kept driving by and sometimes stopping in."

"That must have been pretty hard seeing her," I said, "and hard hearing that she married your best friend."

William Foxwell smiled. "I think she got to have a good life and I'm happy about that," he said. "I think Glenn did, too. I always told him he was the luckiest guy I knew. If there was a dollar bill somebody'd dropped on the ground, you just knew Glenn DeMille would be the one to find it."

Neither one of us said anything for a while. I settled back in bed and let my head drop onto my pillow, figuring we were through talking for the night. I had school in the morning. Those hundred other questions I had for William Foxwell could wait.

But he had other ideas — and more he wanted to say. The visit to Mrs. DeMille had shaken loose all sorts of memories, apparently, and not all of them pleasant.

"I ought to tell you something else I remembered," William Foxwell said. "I didn't want to, but I guess I owe you the truth whenever it comes to me. This ship I was on — I guess it could have been in the Battle of the Coral Sea like you all were talking about. Still not sure. Things are still fuzzy around the edges of that one. But what I remember is a bomb went right down through the middle of the ship. It was an armor-piercing bomb. Tore through everything going down like the ship was made of paper instead of steel, then exploded deep down in the bowels of the ship. Must have killed fifty guys. Maybe more. Probably more. I can't explain how terrible it was. The twisted metal and the boys screaming in pain. The smoke and the fire. The sirens." William paused, as though it hurt to remember that day. Which I guess it probably did.

He continued, "And more bombs falling all around. Antiaircraft guns firing away up at the Japanese planes. I remember I was belowdecks. Can't remember what I was supposed to be doing, or what my job was. But there were officers yelling orders. And so much smoke. Thick black smoke. And awful heat, so strong you couldn't hardly breathe."

"Did you get wounded, or do you think that's where you got, you know . . ." I trailed off.

"Killed?" he asked, finishing my sentence and shaking his head. "Neither one. And kind of worse."

"How could it be worse than getting killed?" I asked.

He looked down. Stared at his hands. The static or whatever it was started up again and he began flickering in and out of view. I couldn't tell if he was losing his voice, too, since he didn't seem to be speaking. I strained to hear him.

"I froze," he said finally.

"What do you mean?" I asked, for some reason thinking he meant that literally — that he turned into ice or something — even though just a minute before he'd been describing the intense heat, and the smoke and the flames from the bombing.

His voice got so soft, less than a whisper, that I could barely hear him. I had to sit up on my bed and lean way forward.

"I mean I froze. I couldn't move. I was so scared when the bombing started that I forgot about everything I was supposed to be doing. It was like I turned deaf to any orders that were meant for me. One of my buddies, he was right next to me one minute, and then the next minute he was down on the floor. I couldn't figure out what was wrong. I mean, he looked just fine at first, until I turned him over and saw . . . there was the jagged end of a metal pipe . . ." He didn't finish.

I shuddered, just to imagine what that must have been like.

"So I hid under some stairs," he went on. "I just curled up there and hid and put my hands over my ears to try to block out all the noise and screaming and bombs and shooting and everything. Only I couldn't, no matter how hard I pressed my hands, until I thought I'd end up crushing my own skull. And maybe I wished I could do that, too."

William Foxwell's voice had grown ragged. I couldn't tell for sure, but he might have been crying, which I didn't think ghosts would do. But there were a lot of things I'd learned about ghosts that didn't fit whatever I might have expected. I wanted to say something to make him feel better, but there was nothing. It was all so terrible, and nothing would change that.

"I'm sorry," he whispered, but whether to me, or to his buddy who died, or to the other men on his ship — because he had gotten so afraid, and because he'd hid under the stairs while they were under attack — I couldn't say.

· · · ·

It was hard concentrating at school the next day. Julie and I sat next to each other during math, in the back, which was a big step for Julie, who'd been a front-row kid ever since I was first aware that she existed. But there was so much we needed to talk about. I had to tell her what William Foxwell had told me the night before, and she had to tell me about her online research, which kept her up half the night. I wasn't sure if it was just the excitement of trying to solve a mystery, or if we were both starting to actually care about the ghost.

"I finally found him," she said excitedly. "William Foxwell. It has to be him because there was only one in the whole database."

"Database of what?" I asked.

"Of casualties," she said. "Or, rather, the part of the database that listed missing in action. They have them for the different wars, but most are World War II. And William Foxwell was in the database for MIA. Only not from the Battle of the Coral Sea. I looked that up, too. But he was MIA from the Battle of Midway. Which didn't happen until a month after Coral Sea."

Julie was so excited when she told me this, that I know it was a disappointment to her that I obviously didn't know that what she'd just said was significant.

She sighed. I didn't even have to ask. "The Battle of Midway was only the most important sea battle in the whole of World War II!" she exclaimed — loud enough, as it turned out, for the teacher to hear us, which got me an extra three sheets of math homework problems, but nothing for Julie, since I think the teacher was kind of afraid of her because she could be so intense and all.

"We'll talk at lunch," Julie said when the bell rang. "Save a table for you and me. And Greg."

"Does he know about any of this?" I asked. "The battle MIA stuff?" I was feeling kind of dumb since I had never heard of the Battle of Midway.

"Oh yeah," Julie said. "We talked last night."

Then she took off for her next class. I just stood there in the hall for a minute, surprised that Julie and Greg were talking — without me. I wasn't jealous, exactly. Just, I don't know, annoyed. I mean, I was the one who found William and tracked down Betty and arranged the road trip to deliver the letter to her. And it was because of me that we had the band, and that Julie got to come along for the ride.

You'd think Julie would be calling me with whatever she found out. Not Greg.

CHAPTER 11

"It totally checks out," Greg said at lunch. None of us had touched the food on our lunch trays. He was talking about what William Foxwell had told me about his ship being hit. "And it *was* the Battle of the Coral Sea, like he mentioned in the letter. There was this ship — a giant aircraft carrier, the *Yorktown*. It got hit by three bombs that the Japanese dropped on them. Some other ships got sunk, but not that one."

Julie practically jumped out of her chair. "That was the same ship he was on when he went missing at the next battle after that — the Battle of Midway!"

I'd never seen her so excited. Everything about Julie

changed as she talked. Her face brightened. She even looked kind of pretty — a totally different person than the one I'd sort of known, at least from a distance, since elementary school.

"Wait a minute," I said, turning my attention back to Greg, who had a big grin on his face, obviously pleased with himself. "You mean to tell me that you, Greg Troutman, were reading up on all this stuff last night? Greg Troutman who hates school? Greg Troutman who never met a homework assignment he didn't try to bribe me into doing for him?"

His grin sagged. He looked annoyed. "Yeah," he said. "That guy. So what?"

"So nothing," I said. "I'm just surprised is all." I hadn't meant to make Greg feel bad. Thankfully, Julie jumped in.

"Never mind him," she said to Greg. "What else did you find out?"

He scowled at me, then spoke very pointedly to Julie, practically elbowing me out of the conversation. "Three bombs, like I said. The Japanese actually thought they'd sunk the *Yorktown*. The worst bomb was just like Anderson said William Foxwell described it. It hit the flight deck and went straight down nearly four decks deep into the ship before it went off. It killed a bunch of the sailors on its way down and when it exploded, but somehow it didn't sink the ship. The *Yorktown* was still in pretty bad shape. There were fires everywhere, and everything was all torn up, all that metal got twisted and ripped apart and stuff."

"What happened then?" I asked. I had decided not to tell them about how William Foxwell said he froze during the battle, after the bomb hit.

Greg shrugged. "Don't know," he said. "That's as far as I got. Maybe we can ask him — William Foxwell. Where is he, anyway? I thought he'd be here."

We all looked around. I still wasn't sure when to expect him to appear, besides, apparently, every night in my bedroom. That didn't stop me from making a guess, though.

"I think he gets tired," I said. "Like, showing himself to us, talking and stuff, trying to remember stuff, it all tires him out. He gets all flickery. And then he disappears and doesn't come around for a while. It's kind of like he has to go recharge his batteries or whatever. Anyway, that's what I think is going on."

"Right," Greg said, not sounding at all sincere. "So you're the ghost expert now?"

"Not an expert," I said, "but I guess I do know him the best of anybody here. I mean, I was the one he showed himself to first, and I'm the one he talks to the most."

Julie sniffed. "Don't be such a snob about this," she said.

"I'm not a snob," I protested. "I'm just trying to help. Anyway, it's not like I can go around telling people I'm friends with a ghost, and that's how I'm going to suddenly be popular in middle school."

"He's right," Greg said, changing his tune. "That's what the band is for, remember?"

"Right," I echoed. "The band."

Julie raised her eyebrows. "The Ghosts of War," she said in a voice that sounded like she was correcting us. I let it go.

"Sure," I said. "Whatever. The Ghosts of War. Rock and roll."

Greg picked up his fork. "We better eat," he said. "We're going to need all our strength for this."

Julie and I both looked at him, waiting for him to elaborate. He shoveled in a mouthful of potatoes and formerly frozen corn.

"*Mmgrmm,*" he said. That was the sound that came out, anyway.

"Gross," Julie said.

Greg's face fell a little as he kept chewing.

"Okay, then," I said. "Band practice this afternoon at

Uncle Dex's. Hopefully, William Foxwell will show back up and we can see what else he remembers."

Greg choked through half his carton of milk, washing down all the potatoes and corn in the process. "That's what I was trying to say in the first place," he said once he could actually talk.

Julie blinked at him. "You really should take smaller bites, you know," she said.

Greg — who just minutes before had seemed like her new best friend or whatever — winced.

Julie was just about to say something else when somebody pulled out a chair next to her and threw himself down in it. It was this eighth grader who everybody just called Belman. I wasn't sure if that was his first name or his last name or what.

Two of his friends dragged out chairs, too. "I'm sorry," Belman said, "but aren't you third graders supposed to be in elementary school? You must have taken the wrong bus. This is middle school. And that's middle school food you're eating."

"Yeah," said one of his friends, reaching for my Jell-O. "And it's for middle school kids only."

The other friend tried to grab Julie's lunch box, but she pulled it away from him.

Greg snatched my Jell-O back from the first guy. "We're not third graders," he said. "And you can't take people's food."

Belman kept this big, weird grin on his face the whole time. "Now, now," he said. "No need to get upset and start crying. Just because you got on the wrong bus this morning."

"Poor little third graders," his first friend said. "Let's let them finish their lunch."

And just like that they got up and moved on to another table where some other sixth graders were sitting. Apparently, they were doing this to everybody who had just started middle school.

"Jerks," Greg said.

"Remember when we used to say that stood for Junior Educated Rich Kids?" I said to him.

Julie sniffed. "Well, it doesn't anymore."

"At least they're doing it to everybody else and not just us," I pointed out, trying to look on the plus side.

Julie brightened. "Well, at least they didn't get these," she said, pulling a small plastic container out of her lunch box. She opened it and handed each of us a cupcake. "I made these last night." She hesitated, and then added, "For you guys."

"Wow," said Greg, as surprised as I was — that Julie would do something nice like that.

We both did our best to thank her but were too busy shoving the cupcakes in our mouths to do it properly. I couldn't be sure about Greg, but I didn't want to risk Belman coming back and stealing mine.

. . . .

William Foxwell didn't show up when we gathered that afternoon for band practice. We'd tortured several songs the week before, and pretty much took up where we'd left off. Julie got frustrated with Greg and me after about ten minutes.

"Do either one of you practice?" she finally snapped. We'd been working on a song of hers, a message song about bullying. The message was supposed to be that bullying is bad, which, of course, everybody already knows, though that doesn't seem to stop it from happening.

Greg admitted that he didn't exactly like to practice on his own. "But isn't that why we're here?" he asked. "To practice?"

I nodded in agreement.

Julie got annoyed. "This is supposed to be *band* practice," she said. "It's not the same thing as *instrument* practice, where you actually try to learn how to play your guitar. It's not just going to happen because you *want* it to happen. You have to *learn*."

Greg and I looked at each other, clearly both thinking the same thing: How could somebody our same age sound so much like a grown-up?

"Let's just try it again," I suggested. "We'll do better, I promise."

"Fine," Julie said. "But promise me you'll practice your instruments when you go home tonight, too. And every night. And every morning. All the time!"

Greg said he was going to start sleeping with his guitar. "I'll probably unplug it from the amp, though," he added. "I don't want to get electrocuted or anything."

"Same here," I said.

Julie threw both hands down on her keyboard. The sound shook the room. "Idiots," she said.

Greg and I just grinned at her.

We launched into the antibullying song again, which seemed appropriate after the incident with Belman and his gang in the lunchroom, and this time almost, sort of, approximately, kind of got it right.

CHAPTER 12

Mom was mad at me when I got home late from practice. She even yelled at me, which she just about never did.

"Anderson Carter, do you know what time it is?"

She was clearly upset with me, but I could also tell that she was in a lot of pain from her MS, and it had probably been a terrible day for her all around. I felt bad, though, that I hadn't checked in with her to see if she needed me to do anything to help.

"Sorry, Mom," I said. "Practice ran late. Do you want me to fix you some dinner or something? Or get you the ice pack?"

Mom sank back into the recliner in the living room, still tense and angry. A vein stood out on her forehead, but I didn't know if that was because of her being mad, or because of how bad she hurt.

"Make yourself something," she said. "Your father's stuck in traffic and won't be home for another hour or so. He just called."

I got Mom some iced tea and cut up an apple and put some cheese and grapes and stuff on a plate, just in case she changed her mind. I hung out with her in the living room, telling her about school and stuff. She felt better after she ate and after she held the cold glass of tea between her hands for a while, sipping occasionally. I told her about band practice and about that song that Julie wrote for us.

"I smell a hit," she said with a small smile.

I hated it when Mom wasn't feeling well, which was a lot of the time. And nothing made me happier than when she started to feel better.

She dismissed me to go do my homework, and so I finally went to my bedroom, dragging my guitar, amp, and book bag with me — and fully expecting William Foxwell to be there. Well, actually I was hoping he would be so I'd have an excuse not to do my math homework. But he didn't show up that night until I finished my last assignment. It was almost as if he'd planned it that way.

"Hey," I said. "Where have you been? Are you okay?" It was funny how quickly I'd gone from being scared out of my mind to being worried about him, the same way I always worried about Mom.

He sat on my bed in his usual place down near the end. The mattress still didn't sag or anything. It was like he was there but he was also *not* there, as weird as that sounds.

"It took me a while," he said.

"What did?" I asked.

He looked around my room, taking in the posters and stuff, as if it was the first time he'd ever been there.

"Putting it all together," he answered. "The story. *My* story. It's like puzzle pieces. There's Betty and Glenn and my old hometown. There's my mom and dad. Enlisting. The war."

"I was going to ask you about that," I said. "You know we won, right? The war, I mean."

He brightened considerably. "Oh yeah?" he said. "I sort of figured we did, from the way you boys were talking. And your friend Julie, well, I can see she's got some Japanese in her, but she was pretty sure about being an American, too."

William Foxwell scratched his chin, and then asked, "How long did it take?"

"The war?" I asked. "World War II?"

"Yeah," he said. "That one."

"About six years," I said. "But the U.S. was just in it for the last four."

William Foxwell shook his head. "That's an awful lot of war."

"Yeah," I agreed. "Too much war."

"I guess any war is too much," he said. "But sometimes you just have to do it. I mean, Hitler and the Nazis. I remember them. And Pearl Harbor and what the Japanese did there."

"You know we're kind of on the same side now," I said. "Us and Japan. We drive a lot of their cars."

William Foxwell's face tightened. "The same side you say? Wow. I'd have never thought that would happen. Who are we up against now? Is it the Germans again? The Soviets?"

I shook my head. "No. Neither one. We're on the same side as the Germans now, too. I mean, we're *friends* with Japan and Germany. And the Soviet Union is called Russia now. Although I'm not too sure about them. We're not exactly *enemies* with the Russians. But I don't think we're what you'd call friends, either."

"Interesting," William Foxwell said. "So I guess it was all worth it in the end. The war, I mean. The one I was in. World War II. There haven't been any others since then, have there?"

"No," I said. "Well, yes. But no *world* wars."

He nodded. "Good," he kept saying. "That's good."

"Yeah," I said. "So, anyway, we did find out some things. Like the name of your ship. And the place where you went missing in action. Were you around when we were talking about it — but just not where we could see you? Usually I feel this weird sort of breeze when I can't see you, but I'm pretty sure you're there."

He sat up straighter on the bed. "No, not this time," he said. "I kind of got hung up." He didn't elaborate.

"Well, anyway, you were on an aircraft carrier ship called the USS *Yorktown*," I said. "First in the Battle of the Coral Sea, which was where your ship got bombed. That's the bombing you told me about the other day. But then a few weeks later you were in an even bigger naval battle called the Battle of Midway. I haven't had time to find out much about that yet, but Julie said she found a record, that that was where you went MIA. She said you were eighteen at that time, and you were a seaman second-class, and you were still serving on the *Yorktown*."

William Foxwell's expression went from quizzical to

dead serious. "Eighteen," he said. "Wow. I mean, I knew I was young and all. But eighteen . . ."

"Do you remember anything about the Battle of Midway?" I asked.

He frowned, wrinkled his brow, obviously thinking hard, trying to remember. "Midway. Midway." He repeated it a few more times, but then seemed to sort of give up. "I'm going to have to think about that one."

Then he brightened. "But I do remember something else about my ship. The *Yorktown*. That sounds right, now that you mention it. Big carrier. Couple thousand of us sailors crammed on board. Months and months at sea. And I remember something else about that Coral Sea battle, too. The Japanese did manage to sink a bunch of our ships. Couple of destroyers, maybe a cruiser, and they nailed us good on the *Yorktown*. But they couldn't sink the *Yorktown* no matter what.

"And I remember us sailing back to Hawaii afterward, with that giant bomb crater gaping open right down the middle of the ship. I couldn't believe we made it. The ocean never looked so big as when we did that. We couldn't repair anything out to sea, so there were the reminders of what happened — right there, everywhere you looked."

"Is there anything else you remember?" I asked, still hoping.

"Now that we're talking about it, yeah, I do," he said. "A few things, anyway. I remember my job was to hose down and clear the flight deck. There were a couple of teams of us. That's what we did morning to night. That and clean and shine anything there was on deck that could be cleaned and shined. There were always oil spills after takeoffs and landings. Those leaky old planes. Or if one of them pancaked a landing, we had to clean that up, too."

"Pancaked a landing?" I said, not sure I heard him right.

"Yeah. An emergency landing," he said. "I sure did wish I could be up in one of those planes instead of scrubbing that darn flight deck. Torpedo plane, dive-bomber, fighter — I didn't care what. I just wished I could somehow get to fly. Pilot or navigator, machine gunner, I didn't care what.

"But that wasn't my job, even though I studied those planes every chance I got, down in the hangar belowdecks. I remember working out in the blazing sun until we were bone tired. Then it was back down below to our bunks, four deep. No, wait. Not bunks. It was hammocks. Wasn't any such thing as privacy. You had your one little shelf and your footlocker stowed down below. And lying there, trying to sleep, there was always so much snoring. Plus, somebody's rear end was always hanging down just above you, practically in your face."

He laughed. "You sure didn't want them serving beans in the mess hall, let me tell you," he said. "Guys in their hammocks, packed in like sardines. Nowhere to get away from a gas attack. And you just know once one fellow started, everybody else was going to answer."

I laughed, too, and that got William Foxwell laughing some more, and once we both got started it was hard to stop. It was good to know some things hadn't changed, and some things never stopped being funny, whether you were in the middle of a world war or not.

·   ·   ·

William Foxwell faded away not too long after that. Maybe all that talking and then laughing wore him out. My eyelids kept drooping shut, so I couldn't say for sure, just that one minute he was there and the next minute he was gone.

The night wasn't over yet, though. I was just about asleep when somebody knocked on my window — three times fast, three times slow, three times fast again, which everybody knows is Morse code for the old distress signal SOS.

I knew right away it was Greg, but it still surprised me. He hadn't done this in a while.

CHAPTER 13

I opened the window and helped Greg climb in.

"Need a place to sleep?" I asked.

He nodded.

"Want to talk about it?" I asked.

He shook his head and I said okay. My sleeping bag was tucked under the bed, and I dragged it out and handed it to him, plus one of my pillows. He threw it on the floor, unzipped the bag, crawled in without bothering to change for bed, and turned his face to the wall.

I heard his muffled voice: "Thanks, Anderson."

"No problem," I said. I knew what it was, of course — his

dad had been drinking. Mostly he didn't drink, according to Greg. But sometimes his dad went into what Greg called his "dark patches" and he drank a lot, usually just for a couple of days. And when that happened, he started yelling at Greg for all kinds of stuff, or for nothing at all. It was never anything more, just the yelling, but that was bad enough for anyone. Greg found it easier if he just stayed out of his dad's way when he was in a dark patch.

Mr. Troutman was pretty quiet most of the time besides that. I could never tell if he liked me or not, but I guess he thought I was okay. Greg and I hung out at my house most of the time, so it wasn't much of an issue. Mr. Troutman had a construction company and hired a lot of war veterans to work for him. He was a war vet, too. Greg said his dad had served in Vietnam. Mom once told me she thought that might have something to do with Mr. Troutman's drinking.

This wasn't the first time Greg had come over to sleep at my house. I'd talked about it before with Mom, and she said it was okay, but not if it became a regular thing. Once, last year, Mr. Troutman came over and talked to Mom after Greg spent the night. He stood on the front porch and wouldn't come in, even though Mom invited him. Mr. Troutman thanked her for being so nice to Greg and apologized. Mom said she hoped he was getting some help and he said he was.

· · ·

Mom was sitting at the table when we came in for breakfast. Dad, who I had never even heard come in last night, had already left again for work.

"Morning, boys," she said.

"Good morning, Mrs. Carter," Greg said. He was always super polite to my parents. He told me one time that he wished they were his. I didn't quite know what to say back.

We wolfed down some cereal and orange juice and rode our bikes to his house to get his books and stuff for school. He had biked over last night without bringing anything, not even a change of clothes. I guess when his dad got going after he'd been drinking, Greg just wanted to get as far away as fast as he could. It helped that I lived only a few blocks away, so it was safe enough for him to ride over.

He was happy to talk about anything else — especially the latest on William Foxwell. I even decided to fill Greg in on how guilty William Foxwell said he still felt — seventy years later — because he did what probably just about anybody would do during a bomb attack on your ship, which was to hide.

"Maybe he, like, redeemed himself later on," Greg said.

"You know, did something heroic, saved somebody's life, something like that."

We were a couple of blocks away from school, still on our bikes, but it looked like we would make it in time for the homeroom bell.

"I don't know," I said. "It would be great if something like that happened. But he told me his job was basically just being a janitor on the ship, cleaning and stuff."

"Well, we have to find out," Greg said. "Or help him find out, or remember. Julie said we need to find out everything we can about this Battle of Midway."

"Oh yeah!" I said, also remembering what Julie had said, and how she had said it: "The Battle of Midway was only the most important sea battle in the whole of World War II!"

• • •

I didn't get a chance to talk to Julie that morning — we had a test, so we weren't allowed to talk for the whole period in the class we had together. I'd studied a little, but not enough. It took me the whole period just to get through by mostly guessing at the answers.

We didn't get a chance to talk during lunch, either, because there was an incident with Greg. Belman showed up in the lunch line and must have said something to him because one minute Greg was just standing there, holding his tray loaded with what looked like mashed potatoes and gravy and more green blobs of quivering Jell-O, and the next minute he was dumping it all onto Belman's shirt. Belman was a lot bigger than Greg. He staggered back with this horrified look on his face, stared at the food smeared all over him and dripping onto the floor, then he grabbed Greg by the front of his shirt and started shaking him like a rag doll, yelling his head off the whole time. "I'll kill you, you little twerp!"

The whole thing lasted only about a minute before one of the vice principals stepped in and broke it up. It was Mr. Crowley, who was also a PE teacher. He wasn't very tall but made up for it by being about twice as wide as any other adult I'd ever seen. He ordered them out of the lunchroom.

Julie had just walked up to my table. "Come on," she said, heading for the door behind them.

"Where?" I asked, reluctant to follow, even though it was Greg.

"To help him, of course," she said, not even bothering to look back at me.

• • •

We stood outside the principal's office and tried to eavesdrop on the conversation — or, rather, the lecture. Principal Lewis was really letting both Greg and Belman have it. I must have heard him say, or shout, "This behavior will not be tolerated at this school!" half a dozen times. Through the door's window I could see Greg just sitting there, fuming, but Belman was slumped down so low that he practically disappeared into his chair.

Julie swallowed hard, and then simultaneously knocked and pushed the door open. Principal Lewis stopped in mid-sentence: "This behavior will not be tol —"

"Sorry, sir," Julie said in her most formal voice. "But we're here as character witnesses."

The principal just stared at her. Nobody ever just walked into Principal Lewis's office like that.

"I'm sure you'll want to hear what we have to say," Julie continued, while the principal remained speechless, though his face had gotten so red — either from yelling at Greg and Belman or because of the interruption — that it seemed not impossible that he might just burst into flames.

Belman sat up straight and glared at Julie.

"We saw the whole thing," Julie added. "Greg was just defending himself. I'm sure he feels terrible for letting his emotions get the better of him, but some things you shouldn't be allowed to say at school, and I don't think they should even be repeated here in your office." Then, she cut her eyes at Belman.

I was certain that there was no way for Julie to know what Belman had actually said to Greg, but it didn't matter in the end. Principal Lewis sputtered for a moment but didn't ask for specifics.

"Back to your classes!" he barked at all of us. "And don't let me hear about any more disturbances. This behavior will not be tolerated in this school. Am I clear?"

"Yes, sir," said Julie. She yanked Greg up, and we took off before Principal Lewis could change his mind. Belman wasn't so lucky.

"Not so fast, young man," the principal snapped when he tried to follow us. "You'd been warned already not to show your face back in my office."

The door closed behind us, and we practically raced down the hall to grab books from our lockers and make it to the next class.

· · ·

I told Julie later that I figured Belman had said something about Greg's dad. It had happened before. Ever since I was first friends with Greg, people would see his dad somewhere after he'd been drinking, and then they'd make fun of him when they saw Greg. Greg couldn't stand it when anybody did that.

It was one thing for him to complain about his dad to me or whatever, but it was another for somebody else to say something.

Twice I'd had to help Greg out when he went after a bigger guy, like Belman in the lunchroom. Both times I tackled the guy off Greg — even though I was so scared my teeth were actually chattering — and then Greg and I went running away before the guy could get up.

This time, though, it was something different. Greg clued us in when he came to band practice that afternoon.

"He said he heard we were starting a band," Greg explained, "and he said we were the three loseriest kids in school. That's actually how he said it: 'loseriest.' I don't even think that's a real word. What an idiot."

"And you dumped your lunch on him for that?" Julie asked.

Greg looked away. "He might have said some other things," he said. "But, hey, why don't we get started on practice, anyway? I've been working on the vocals for that bullying song, and I'm ready to wail."

I laughed when he said "ready to wail." It sounded like an old eighties expression my dad might use to sound cool.

Greg plugged his guitar into his amplifier, and Julie and I did the same with my guitar and her keyboard.

I thought for a second I heard a trumpet playing off somewhere down the hall — just for a second — but then nothing.

CHAPTER 14

Greg came home with me after practice, but he still wouldn't tell me what Belman had said in the lunchroom. I finally gave up, and we decided to get on the Internet and look up the Battle of Midway. Even history research beat doing homework, as far as Greg was concerned.

What we found out was a lot.

There was a bunch of stuff online about how powerful the Imperial Japanese Navy was, and how pathetic the U.S. fleet was in comparison, especially after the Japanese sneak attack on Pearl Harbor.

The Americans and the Australians might have stopped

the Japanese at Coral Sea, where the *Yorktown* got bombed so badly, but the Imperial Navy, with their battleships and aircraft carriers and deadly submarines and superior airplanes and pilots, were definitely kicking butt everywhere else.

Especially because of their fighter planes — the famous Japanese Zeroes — that were so much faster than anything the U.S. had in the air. The way the Internet explained it, because they were so fast it was easy for the Zeroes to shoot down U.S. bomber planes whenever we tried to attack Japanese ships.

"Man," Greg said at one point, letting out a long whistle. "I never realized how much better than us they were."

"Yeah," I said. "We were getting totally schooled."

Greg and I wrestled for the mouse so we could keep on clicking and reading.

"So let me get this straight," Greg said after we read some more. "It was basically two wars we were fighting at once: the one in Europe against the Nazis and the one in the Pacific against the Japanese. And early on we were losing both?

"And look at this," Greg said before I could answer. He pointed to a page on one of the history websites we'd found. "We were afraid of the Japanese attacking Hawaii again and finishing off the job they started at Pearl Harbor."

I pointed to the paragraph after the one he was exclaiming about. "*And* we were afraid that they would attack California, too."

We both just sat there for a minute, letting this all sink in.

"So what about the Battle of Midway?" Greg asked.

"I think we're getting to that," I said. "But what I want to know first is where in the world Midway is even located."

We pulled up some maps and pored over them until Greg shouted, "There it is!"

"Where?" I asked, squinting. The spot he was pointing at was barely a dot on the map. I leaned closer and squinted harder at the dot, and the writing next to it, and sure enough, there it was: Midway Islands. Right in the middle of the Pacific Ocean, halfway between Japan and California, more than a thousand miles north of the Hawaiian Islands.

Somebody cleared his throat behind us, and Greg and I both jumped out of our chairs.

It was William Foxwell.

"It isn't actually an island," he said, as if he'd been in on the conversation all along. And who knows? Maybe he had been, just listening and not saying anything. He didn't exactly make a lot of noise when he moved around. Definitely no clanking chains or spooky winds or creaking doors.

"What is it, then?" Greg asked.

"It's what you call an atoll," William Foxwell said. "I remember we heard about it. We had an airbase there. The Japanese wanted it to use for their next attack on Pearl Harbor. And they wanted our boys gone."

"Right," Greg said. "And an atoll is what exactly?"

"Kind of a coral reef ring with a big lagoon in the middle. The islands where the bases are, they're part of the atoll."

"What about the Battle of Midway?" I asked. "Do you remember that now, too, and what happened on your ship?"

William Foxwell nodded. "Kind of. Some of it. There's a lot that's still so fuzzy. But yeah. I remember now after the Coral Sea battle, after we made it back to Hawaii on the *Yorktown*, they brought a whole army of workers on board for emergency repairs. They had the entire crew working, too. And if we couldn't repair something, they had us just nail up thick sheets of wood or steel and wall it off. Nobody even got any leave to go ashore. We were told it would take three months, that we'd be out of commission too long to help out at Midway. But the admiral said the *Yorktown* was getting fixed no matter what — and not in three months but in *three days*! He said she was going out to battle no matter what."

"The admiral?" Greg asked.

"Admiral Chester Nimitz," William Foxwell said, with an admiring tone in his voice. "The old man."

"So he was, like, in charge, or whatever?" Greg asked.

"Oh yeah," William Foxwell said, nodding emphatically. "Definitely the one in charge."

"So what happened?" I asked.

William Foxwell smiled. "What do you think happened? The old man said to get the *Yorktown* repaired and join up with the rest of the fleet at Midway, so that's what happened. Of course, nobody was supposed to know anything about where we were going and what was up. It was all top secret. But we knew all the same. My buddy Dewey Tomzak told me about it. He heard it from a guy down in the engine room. Don't know where the engine-room guy heard it, but once somebody did, everybody did.

"Dewey said there was a rumor that we had a bunch of genius math guys in a secret bunker monitoring all the Japanese radio communications," he continued, "and those boys managed to crack the Japanese radio code and that's how we knew they were going after Midway. And that's how the old man knew where to set his trap. Except we had only two other *Yorktown*-class carrier ships, ones that could hold a whole lot of planes — just two in the whole entire fleet, I'm pretty sure — so it was why they needed the *Yorktown* so bad."

I'd been scanning the history website while he talked, and so far everything he said matched up: What William Foxwell hadn't said — and maybe didn't know, and maybe never knew — was that the Imperial Japanese Navy armada steaming across the Pacific was the most powerful naval force in history!

Greg was peppering William Foxwell with a bunch of other questions about Midway, but I could tell William's gas gauge was close to empty, or his battery was running down, or whatever it was that happened to him when he began fading out, and his memory stopped working.

And then there was a quick knock on my bedroom door, the door swinging open before I could answer. It was Dad, who seemed to have a habit of interrupting just when things were getting the most interesting.

"Hey, boys. Time for dinner."

William Foxwell had already disappeared.

My head was spinning with all we'd just learned. It was hard being with William Foxwell one minute, and finding all this stuff out about what happened to him, and in the war, seventy years ago, and then suddenly being back in the real world.

Dad asked Greg if he'd like to come with us. We were going out for cheeseburgers because Mom was asleep on the couch in the living room and Dad didn't want us to disturb her.

"Yes, sir," Greg said quickly. "I'd like to."

"And spending the night again?" Dad asked, as if that was a normal thing, which I suppose it kind of was.

"If that's okay," Greg said.

Dad looked at his watch. "Sure it is," he said. "Let's just call your dad so he'll know where you are."

Greg said he would, though he went outside to do it on his cell phone.

CHAPTER 15

Julie went one step further than Greg and me and actually checked out some books on the Battle of Midway from the library. Greg and I both felt that if you couldn't find it on the Internet, why bother? But when we said that to Julie, she just rolled her eyes and said, "Information is only as good as its source."

"But the Internet is so easy!" Greg told her, and I had to agree. Plus, it had gotten us all the way to sixth grade and hadn't let us down yet. So far, so good.

Julie rolled her eyes again, and handed each of us a book. "Morons," she said. "Read these, and report back tomorrow.

If you can find the entire book online, you can read it there. We need to know everything."

Greg couldn't believe it. "A whole book in one night?" he wailed. "Not possible!"

I said pretty much the same thing, but I knew there was no use arguing with Julie.

"Look," she said, "you might have both seen him last night, but I just have a feeling that we don't have all the time in the world to find out what happened to him. We have to get serious about this, or else I'm afraid William Foxwell will be stuck like he was for all those years since the war."

"You mean, like, forever?" Greg asked.

"Maybe," Julie said. "It could be. I mean, what are the rules here? It's like there are Newton's laws, physical laws, all of which we can verify and understand."

"Sort of," Greg said.

"Not sort of," Julie said. "Definitely. So how does it work with ghosts? Anderson can see him and talk to him when he's by himself. Anderson was the first one that the ghost revealed himself to. I only saw him, or the idea of him, or whatever that was, when he visited Anderson at the cafeteria that day. But to the rest of the kids in the lunchroom it just probably looked like Anderson was talking to himself."

"Not probably," Greg said. "That jerk kid Belman said something about it. He asked me if Anderson was mentally challenged or mentally ill or something."

"What?" I said. "You didn't tell me that before."

Greg looked down. "I didn't want to hurt your feelings," he said.

"Too late for that now," Julie said.

She waited for about a second, then changed the subject back to ghosts in general, and William Foxwell in particular.

"It is only a theory," she said, picking up where she'd left off, "but what I think is that there is an energy. That energy was awakened when Anderson found the coat and the letter, and at first, once it was awakened, that energy was very strong. So strong that Anderson could hear William Foxwell and see him. So strong that he could follow Anderson, and even show himself to us, to Anderson's friends."

I was getting the picture. "So strong that he could lift some things and hold them — the letter and the coat?" I asked.

"Right," Julie said. "And the trumpet. The letter and the coat, these had great meaning for him. So the energy was strong. I'm not so sure about the trumpet."

"Maybe that had great meaning for him, too," I said. "Not

that particular trumpet, but playing the trumpet. Maybe he played in the high school band?"

"Yes. That's right. That could be it," Julie said, pausing and nodding.

Then she continued, "So, anyway, the energy was so strong at first, but my theory is that there is a limited amount of this energy, and once it is awakened, it can only exist for a certain time, and then no more."

It was my turn to start nodding in agreement. This made a lot of sense. "And that's why William Foxwell is only coming to see me every so often now," I interjected. "And why he fades in and out sometimes, and his voice gets hard to hear, and he can sometimes listen in on what we're saying, but not be a part of the conversation or show himself to us. Stuff like that."

"Yes," Julie said. "At least, that is my theory. And I think that maybe the energy that is William Foxwell — his ability to talk to us — might be running out. And if we don't have the answer for him soon, we may never be able to solve his mystery for him so that he can find his peace."

Greg grabbed one of the books Julie had checked out of the library. "Well then, what are we waiting for?" he asked. "Let's start reading already."

I nearly burst out laughing. Those were definitely not words I thought I'd ever hear coming from Greg.

At the same time I felt a kind of panic or nausea or something in the pit of my stomach. What if Julie was right? What if we were running out of time to help William Foxwell right when we just seemed to be getting started? Everything that Julie said made sense, scary as it was, and as much as I didn't want to believe it.

And then another thing struck me. Listening to Julie talk, and seeing how much thought she'd put into figuring all this out, and also seeing how much Greg cared about what happened to William Foxwell — it all made me realize something. I had been thinking that William Foxwell was sort of, well, *my* friend, but I could see now that Greg and Julie must be feeling the same way about him.

After that, we got back down to the business of dividing up the books.

Julie's was about what the Japanese were up to in their plans to attack Midway. Mine told the American side of the story. And lucky Greg, he had a short autobiography of a navy pilot who was the only man in his torpedo bomber squad who survived the U.S. attacks on the Japanese aircraft carriers. It was called *Sole Survivor*.

I felt my stomach sink.

CHAPTER 16

William Foxwell didn't show up that night, which made me worry even more about what Julie had said. I finished my homework and practiced my guitar for a while, then dove into my assigned reading, which I didn't mind at all because I knew it might help us help William Foxwell, and, of course, just because it was history.

The story began with the now familiar account of the Japanese attack on Pearl Harbor, and their plans to control the Pacific Rim. And they were well on their way to doing it after Pearl Harbor, too.

I shuddered when I read about the Battle of the Coral Sea and the armor-piercing bomb that one of the Japanese planes dropped on the *Yorktown*'s deck — just the way William Foxwell described it. The book talked about all the men who were killed and wounded and horribly burned, and I wondered how many of them had been his friends, and how awful that must have been for him and for those guys' families.

But at least their families knew what happened to them — that they had fought bravely and been heroes. And I guessed that meant they could rest easy in heaven or whatever, after they died. Not like William Foxwell, who still felt so guilty because he froze and hid during the battle, and then went missing somehow in the Battle of Midway. He was still missing in action, in a way.

I continued reading deep into the night. Another whole chapter on the guys who broke the Japanese code, and how, even though they were able to decipher a lot of the Japanese radio communications and stuff, they weren't able to figure out everything. It was like only hearing every third or fourth word of a conversation, or worse — encrypted, in Japanese. So there was still some guessing involved when they told Admiral Nimitz about the Japanese plans to attack Midway.

And there was another complication. Admiral Nimitz knew that everything the code-breakers had deciphered might have been a total Japanese ruse — fake information planted to trick the U.S. into *thinking* the attack was on Midway, when really they were planning to attack somewhere else altogether.

But Admiral Nimitz listened to the code-breakers and decided that the best bet was to be lying in wait somewhere out of sight near Midway when the Imperial Navy showed up, and then hit them in a giant sneak attack using all the American torpedo bombers and dive-bombers and anything else they could fit onto our aircraft carriers.

That was going to be a lot easier said than done, of course, and Admiral Nimitz knew it. The Japanese had so many more ships and planes than the U.S. that the whole plan struck a lot of Admiral Nimitz's advisers as practically suicidal. Especially because the U.S. didn't even have any *battleships* anymore, with all their big guns and cannons and stuff to fight a big naval battle. They had all been destroyed or damaged in the attack on Pearl Harbor six months before.

Meanwhile, the gargantuan Japanese force steaming toward Midway was the same force — most of the same ships, most of the same officers, most of the same bomber and fighter pilots, most of the same everything — responsible for the sneak attack on Pearl Harbor.

Admiral Nimitz knew the U.S. had only one chance, and that was to first let the Japanese attack the island of Midway — the *atoll* of Midway! — and let them think the American fleet was nowhere around. Knowing the enemy was coming, the navy and the marines set up all the defenses they could on Midway in preparation for the attack, which they knew would come in waves. The first wave would be the Japanese fighters and bombers from their aircraft carriers, bombing the military area to keep the U.S. distracted and out of the sky. The second wave, if the battle got that far, would be the Japanese bombarding Midway from their battleships in preparation for a huge land invasion.

Admiral Nimitz, and everybody else on our side, knew there was no way for us to win if that happened.

The only thing that could save us, and maybe even save the whole war, was if U.S. planes could take off from our hidden aircraft carriers to counterattack the Japanese ships — after the Japanese planes returned from their bombing mission on Midway, but before that second wave of the Japanese assault could get started.

There wouldn't be much time, and everything had to go exactly right if we were going to have a chance of stopping them and maybe, just maybe, turning around the war.

I read for as long as I could, until my eyes wouldn't stay open any longer, no matter what I did to try to make myself stay awake. I finally fell asleep around two o'clock in the morning and when I did I had this crazy dream where I was on a little boat in the middle of the Pacific Ocean. All around me were big ships and airplanes landing and taking off on their decks. Greg was right next to me, of course. He was steering and I was looking over the side, hoping nobody dropped any bombs on us or torpedoes or anything, and meanwhile trying to find William Foxwell in the middle of all of the chaos of battle.

I still hadn't been able to find him when I woke up the next morning for school, and it bothered me all day.

CHAPTER 17

Julie had made cupcakes again, and Greg and I scarfed ours down first thing at lunch the next day. No telling if Belman would be back, or what he and his friends would try to take from us. I made sure to thank Julie first this time. She even smiled at me.

As soon as his mouth wasn't full anymore, Greg started talking about his book, which picked up the story where I had left off reading in mine — with the U.S. counterattack on the Japanese aircraft carriers.

"So this American pilot, the sole survivor, his name was George Gay and he was from Texas," Greg said. He paused to lick icing off his fingers. "And the plane he flew, it was a torpedo bomber. They called the torpedo bombers 'Devastators,' which I thought was awesome until I read some more about how ridiculously slow they were, and how bad their aim was with their bombs." He paused to take another bite of cupcake.

"And once they made it to their targets, in order to fire their torpedoes they had to slow down even more," Greg added after swallowing. "They had to fly just barely above the ocean waves, so when the bombardiers finally released their bombs, the torpedoes would keep gliding fast through the water and keep going until they hit the side of whatever ship they were supposed to be aimed at."

"Bombardiers?" Julie asked.

"Yeah," said Greg. "They were the guys who would crawl into this really small space on the underside of the Devastators, where they would have to lie facedown and look through a little window at whatever was underneath the plane. They pulled a lever or something to let their bomb go when they thought they were lined up right to hit their target. Meanwhile, there was the pilot flying the plane, of course. And a guy with a mounted machine gun in a cockpit behind the pilot. He was supposed to protect the plane from enemy fighters — those Japanese Zeroes.

"Only, in the Battle of Midway, nearly all the TBDs —
which was also what they called the torpedo bombers — either
got shot down by the Zeroes or by the Japanese antiaircraft
guns on the Imperial Navy ships. If they somehow managed
to survive all that, most of them still ended up crashing into
the ocean because they ran out of fuel, or because their steering mechanisms were so shot up that they couldn't make it
back to Midway or to one of the U.S. aircraft carriers that
they had flown from."

"Wow," I said. "Greg, man, you're starting to sound like
an encyclopedia or something."

He took it as a compliment and went on. He had apparently read his whole entire book in one night, which was
definitely some sort of record.

"George Gay said the pilots and their machine gunners
and their bombardiers actually knew, before they took off,
that they probably didn't have enough fuel to make it back,"
he said. "They had to fly, like, a couple of hundred miles, to
find the Japanese ships, drop their bombs, and try to make
it all the way back, even though everybody knew that wasn't
going to happen. But they all went anyway."

Julie asked if George Gay was on William Foxwell's ship,
the *Yorktown*, but it turned out he wasn't. "His ship was the

Hornet," Greg said. "There was the *Hornet* and the *Enterprise*. Those were the first ships to send out their bombers. The *Yorktown* sent theirs out last."

"So what happened?" I asked. "They sunk the Japanese ships, right?"

"Wrong," Greg and Julie said at the same time.

Greg continued, "Not one of them — not a single, solitary one of the Devastators, and there were dozens of them that launched from the American aircraft carriers — managed to hit a Japanese ship with their torpedoes. Their main targets were these four Japanese aircraft carriers. None got so much as a scratch. At least not from the Devastators."

"What about George Gay and his torpedo bomber?" I asked.

Greg shook his head and stirred around some of his lunch with his fork. "After George Gay missed with his bomb — even though he thought he was dead on target — he got shot down, too. His machine gunner and bombardier were both killed. But George Gay survived. He was the only one in his whole squadron who did."

"So he really was the sole survivor, like the title of his book?" I said.

"Yeah," Greg replied.

He went on to tell us how George Gay somehow managed to stay alive the entire rest of the naval battle, too — fourteen long hours, including one very long, lonely night, at sea — by hiding under a seat cushion from his plane. Even though Japanese ships were constantly going past him and he could hear their sailors shouting. "It was a miracle one of them didn't run him over," Greg said. "Anyway, he was finally rescued by a U.S. scout plane — a seaplane — after the fighting ended, though a lot of Japanese ships were still close by in the area."

Greg stabbed at some corn on his lunch tray, but the kernels just rolled to the side. "It's like something out of a movie," he said. "I mean, the U.S. was so much weaker than the Japanese fleet and all. It was like David and Goliath. They already kicked our butt, and they were coming in with this enormous fleet of ships to finish off the job. The U.S. was all wobbly, but then got this secret information about what was about to happen. And then they set this ambush. But then they got their butts kicked all over again."

"Yeah, I know, right?" I said, picking up where Greg left off. "And did you read the part where the Japanese also attacked Alaska, of all places, at the same time, to try to fake out the Americans about what they were actually after?"

Greg hadn't, but Julie had. "Of course, the cryptanalysts

had deciphered that information as well from the coded communications," she said.

Greg blinked. "Could you say that again in English?"

Even Julie had to laugh. "The code-breakers," she explained. "They knew that, too, and told Admiral Nimitz. So the U.S. could be ready for the attack on those Alaskan island bases, but didn't send their ships there. The Japanese never knew any of this, of course. They thought they had the element of surprise."

Once again the bell rang, interrupting us. I couldn't believe how quickly lunch was over — and none of us seemed to have eaten a thing. My stomach rumbled as I carried my tray to drop it off on the conveyor belt that sent it back to the kitchen, and I knew I was going to be hungry all afternoon.

Julie, Greg, and I agreed to meet up after school for band practice — and to fill one another in on the rest of what we'd read — and then we took off in three different directions.

I wished William Foxwell had been there to hear everything we'd been talking about. I wondered if one of the reasons he hadn't been around so much lately was because maybe he was already starting to remember a lot of this stuff himself. On one hand, I hoped so. On the other hand, I really wanted to be the one to tell him.

CHAPTER 18

In the middle of sixth period

that day, I remembered something, or rather someone, who was probably the biggest clue we'd been given since Betty Corbett. It was William Foxwell's friend on the *Yorktown* — Dewey Tomzak — the guy who had told him about the secret U.S. plan for the Battle of Midway. I couldn't believe we hadn't already tried to find him and ask if he knew what happened to William Foxwell.

I wanted to kick myself for forgetting such an important clue. Some kind of history detective I was turning out to be. I wrote the name down in my notebook before I could forget it again — *Dewey Tomzak* — and couldn't wait to get to band practice that afternoon to tell Julie and Greg.

. . .

They were as excited as I was when we met up at the Kitchen Sink, although once Greg and I finished high-fiving each other, Julie gave us a lecture about how we should start writing everything down so we wouldn't forget any more important things.

I showed her my notebook. "Already did," I said, but she just rolled her eyes.

We spent the next ten minutes trying in vain to get Internet reception in the basement. When that didn't work, we went upstairs, where we could actually pick up the Wi-Fi connection. Julie went right to work looking up Dewey Tomzak on her phone.

Uncle Dex was curious, of course. "And why are you trying to find this guy?" he asked.

"It's for school," I said, as if I actually thought that would be enough for Uncle Dex.

"And what's his name again?" he asked.

I told him. "He was kind of famous in World War II," I lied.

Uncle Dex frowned. "Never heard of him. But, hey, I'll see what I can find, too." He got busy on his own computer at the counter. There were just a couple of people in the store, but neither one looked as if they were actually interested in buying anything. They might as well have had the words "Just looking around" tattooed on their foreheads.

"Found something!" Uncle Dex shouted after a few minutes. Julie looked annoyed. She clearly didn't like anybody beating her at anything, including Internet searches.

"Wow!" Uncle Dex exclaimed. "He was on the *Yorktown* with your old pal, William Foxwell. Another seaman second-class. This says he was honorably discharged after the war."

"Does it say where he lives?" I asked. "Does it give his address or say where he was from or if he's still alive — stuff like that?"

"No address," Uncle Dex said. "He was from Harrisburg, Pennsylvania, when he joined the navy. But that was a long time ago."

"We know," Julie said. Then, to me and Greg, she said, "I found him, too." She smiled a sort of triumphant smile. "*And* I found a Dewey Tomzak who still lives in Harrisburg."

Nobody wanted to look at Uncle Dex and invite any more questions. Julie put her phone in her back pocket, and we all trooped back down to the basement to figure out what we should do next.

Julie thought we should call Dewey Tomzak right away, but I didn't want to risk Uncle Dex getting suspicious.

"I'm not sure he totally bought into that war hero stuff," I said. "And I can't exactly tell him we're doing all this because of a ghost."

Julie poked my arm with her index finger. "You explained it to *us*," she said.

"Well," said Greg, "technically it was the ghost himself who explained it to us, so it's kind of different. I mean, we could see him, so, you know, once we got finished freaking out it all made sense. Sort of."

We decided we'd wait until Uncle Dex left for the day, then go upstairs to call Dewey Tomzak. Meanwhile, Julie said she had a new song to teach us. It wasn't one of her originals, as it turned out. Instead it was a really old song neither Greg nor I had ever heard of, but that apparently used to be popular a long time ago. Julie knew about it from her dad, who seemed to know a lot of weird and obscure American songs. It was called "How Can I Miss You When You Won't Go Away?"

Uncle Dex must have heard us practicing — or else he came down to eavesdrop. However it happened, he came bursting into the practice room with his ukulele and a small amplifier, "ready to jam," as he put it.

The next thing we knew, Julie and Uncle Dex had pretty much taken over the song, while Greg and I struggled through the chord progression that Julie had printed out for us. Greg, who was our lead singer, or was supposed to be, anyway, tried to both sing and play the new song but had to concentrate too hard on the music, so Uncle Dex took over singing. Julie didn't seem to mind, but Greg and I cringed — especially when Uncle Dex started yodeling. I actually shuddered. Greg did, too.

"Well," Uncle Dex said after we ran through it a couple of times, "guess it's time for me to close up shop." And with that, he packed up his uke and amp and clomped back upstairs.

"Don't forget to lock up behind you," he yelled back to me. He had given me a key after forgetting he had to lock up that first time Greg and I were down there.

After he left, we went upstairs and called the number for Dewey Tomzak in Harrisburg, Pennsylvania. I put my phone on speaker so everybody could hear, but we agreed that I would do all the talking.

"Hello?" an elderly man's voice answered on the first ring. I wasn't prepared for that, but I guess some people are just always sitting with their phones, waiting for somebody to call.

"Yes, sir," I said. "Hello, sir. Is this Mr. Tomzak? Mr. Dewey Tomzak from World War II?"

Julie and Greg both smacked their foreheads at the stupid thing I had just said. I wanted to smack my own forehead, too.

"What's that you say?" the man asked.

"I'm sorry," I said. "Is this Mr. Tomzak? My name is Anderson Carter, and I'm trying to get in touch with Mr. Dewey Tomzak. It's for a school project. About World War II. That's what I meant to say."

There was a short pause. And then, "Yes. Yes. This is Dewey Tomzak. Now what's this about again? Is this a solicitation? You want money for what?"

"No, sir," I said. "We're not looking for money. I was looking for someone named Dewey Tomzak who was in the navy."

"Yes," he said. "I was in the navy. And who is this again?"

I introduced myself again and explained that I was in middle school in Virginia and working on a history project for one of my classes. "I found a navy peacoat and an old letter belonging to a man — a sailor who I believe served with you on the *Yorktown*. I was hoping you might be able to give me some information about him. About what happened to him."

Mr. Tomzak seemed to be breathing kind of hard all of a sudden. I asked if he was okay and he said he was, but he needed to sit down in his chair to finish the conversation. I heard his footsteps and then the sounds of him sinking into a chair. I even heard him pull the lever so it leaned back. It was kind of a loud chair. It occurred to me that getting a phone call like this might be a pretty big deal for Mr. Tomzak — a pretty big deal for anybody who had fought in the war a long time ago.

"Okay," he said. "Now who's this sailor you're calling about. You say we were on the same ship? On the *Yorktown*? You know that was a doomed ship, don't you?"

"Yes, sir," I said, although I hadn't read enough yet about the rest of the Battle of Midway to actually know that. It sent a chill up my spine when he said it.

"The name of this fellow?" he asked again. "You were just saying?"

I took a deep breath and then told him: "William Foxwell."

There was another long pause, and then a whistling sound — which I guess was Mr. Tomzak whistling. And then he said, "William Foxwell. Well, I'll be."

CHAPTER 19

"You know, I didn't like him at first," Mr. Tomzak said. "When I was a boy I lived in Philadelphia, and anybody who had a Southern accent like Foxy — that's what we all called him — I just figured they must be a dumb hillbilly."

He laughed. "Of course, that was just prejudiced and Foxy was nothing of the sort," he continued. "And it turned out, he thought I must be one of those pushy, obnoxious Northerners because of *my* accent. But that's the great thing about the service. It put a lot of us fellows together from all over, and we got to see that once you get past how somebody talks, or what they like to eat, or what sports team they root for, we're all pretty much the same. Every one of us on the *Yorktown*, I'd have to say we were all good Americans. We were all proud to serve our country."

I liked when Mr. Tomzak said that. And I bet William Foxwell must have felt the same way.

Mr. Tomzak laughed again. "Another thing we had in common was we all hated the food on board and couldn't wait for shore leave so we could get some real food. That was the worst thing about returning to Hawaii after that Battle of the Coral Sea. Here we all thought we were going to get us some shore leave and everything that came with it, and instead nobody got to leave the ship. We were all too busy helping with the repairs, getting ready for Midway!"

I asked how well he had known William Foxwell and Mr. Tomzak said pretty well. "I heard so much about his girl back home I was about ready to marry her myself," he said. "Of course, I didn't have a girl of my own at the time, so I was envious of anybody who did. Especially somebody like Foxy with a girl that pretty." He gave a small chuckle before continuing, "He used to show me her picture all the time."

I smiled, thinking about Betty Corbett and William Foxwell way back then.

Mr. Tomzak cleared his throat and started talking again. "I'll tell you what else I knew about Foxy. I knew that more than anything he wanted to be a navy pilot up in one of our fighter planes. Or if not a pilot, then a bombardier or machine gunner on one of those torpedo bombers. Heck, even a scout plane. He didn't care. He must have put in applications for flight school once a month, even though he knew they wouldn't even process that many requests. Plus, he hadn't finished high school, so there was no way he'd be accepted. But Foxy just kept hoping they'd get desperate for him. The painful truth was he wasn't going anywhere. But he still dreamed about it."

It made me sad to hear that. As bad as he wanted to fly and all, I bet William Foxwell would have been a great pilot.

Mr. Tomzak said every chance Foxy had he would climb up on the planes on the flight deck or down belowdecks in the hangars to check out the instrument panels, the guns, everything. And he asked questions so much of the pilots and the other members of the flight crews that they tried to avoid Foxy any time they saw him coming.

"He got us in trouble a couple of times," Mr. Tomzak said. "Dragging me over with him to examine something or other on those dive-bombers and torpedo bombers and all when we were supposed to be doing our jobs keeping the flight deck cleaned and all that grunt work they had us do."

I asked Mr. Tomzak where he was when the *Yorktown* got bombed in the Battle of the Coral Sea, and was he with William Foxwell.

"No," he said. "I was in my bunk at the time. I'd come down with something or other. Don't know where Foxy was, but I do know we lost some of our friends. He took it really hard. We all did, of course, but he seemed to take it the hardest. He wouldn't talk about what happened, but for a long time after that, most of a week, he wouldn't hardly talk to me or anybody."

"Then what?" I asked, working my way up to asking about how Mr. Tomzak thought William Foxwell went missing at the Battle of Midway. Julie and Greg were crowded next to me the whole time I was on the phone with Mr. Tomzak, actually pressed against me as though we were having a group hug.

"You mean what happened to Foxy?" Mr. Tomzak said. "I surely wish I knew, and I've wondered about it all these years. Everything was so busy when we got to Hawaii, fixing up the ship during those three days in port, and then taking off right away for Midway. I hardly had time to say hello to

Foxy or anybody else for that matter. All I can tell you is that once we got in position at Point Luck — that was what they called the rendezvous site where our ships were hiding out near Midway — it was all business and total chaos. Well, a kind of controlled chaos."

I tried to imagine it, and kept picturing that scene from the dream I had where Greg and I were in that little boat in the middle of everything, looking for William Foxwell.

Mr. Tomzak continued, "Everybody knew where they were supposed to be and what they were supposed to be doing, but that doesn't mean that it all happened smoothly. That's about the best way I can put it. I remember Foxy at one point racing belowdecks to get to the head right before they gave the order for our torpedo bomber squads to take off. They were bringing all the planes up from the hangar belowdecks on these giant elevators. The pilots and their crews came out in their flight suits and headgear. One fellow, a machine gunner, I remember came running out real late. His plane was already taxiing over, lining up for takeoff when he climbed in.

"I don't remember Foxy coming back on deck, but he must have at some point. It's just that once things got going and those planes started taking off, I didn't notice much of anything. And then, once all the planes took off, we had to clear the deck and get into our battle stations in case the Japanese found us and attacked us with their planes.

He paused and took a deep breath. "And I never saw Foxy again."

Mr. Tomzak coughed into the phone again. I realized he must be pretty old, probably in his nineties, and here we were asking him to remember — and to relive — what happened in the war, and what happened to his friend who disappeared and didn't survive. I wondered if Mr. Tomzak was even crying a little, which made me feel bad.

I apologized for bringing all this stuff up, but Mr. Tomzak insisted that it was okay. "No need to apologize at all," he said. "Sometimes it's good to talk about it. You have to remember. It's when everybody starts forgetting that you get in trouble."

"Forgetting what, Mr. Tomzak?" I asked.

He seemed surprised by my question. "Why, how terrible it all was. The terrible things we do to one another in war. How young we all were, us and the Japanese, and what an awful waste of so many young lives."

·   ·   ·

Julie, Greg, and I walked home quietly after the phone call with Mr. Tomzak. He couldn't tell us anything else about

William Foxwell, and I think we were all feeling sad, and feeling like the war — Mr. Tomzak's war and William Foxwell's war — was starting to seem like it was our war, too.

There was still so much we didn't know about the Battle of Midway, and what happened to the *Yorktown*, and, of course, what happened to William Foxwell. But what we did know felt almost like too much. After a few blocks, we all went our separate ways, hardly even saying good-bye.

Mom asked me at dinner if I was feeling okay. I guess I wasn't saying much there, either. Dad was home for once and after I assured Mom that I was fine, Dad and Mom got distracted talking about some weekend plans they had to go up to the mountains on Skyline Drive and see the leaves changing color. Mom had been feeling a little better lately and thought she was up for it. I told them I had been at band practice — that the All-Ages Open Mic Night was soon and we wanted to be in it.

"What's the name of your band again?" Dad asked. "The Great Beyond? The Afterlife? Something like that?"

"Close," I said. "It's the Ghosts of War."

I excused myself from the table shortly after and headed for my bedroom. William Foxwell still wasn't there. It had been a couple of days since I'd seen him, and I was definitely starting to worry now. I forced myself to sit down and crank through my homework, and then I made a list of the things I still needed to find out about the Battle of Midway.

What happened after the Japanese shot down all the torpedo bombers?

How did we still manage to win the Battle of Midway?

And what did Dewey Tomzak mean when he said the *Yorktown* was "a doomed ship"?

I clearly had a lot more reading to do. But even with that, I was going to have to wait for William Foxwell to show up again and hope it would all be enough to stimulate his memory so we could find out the rest of his story.

CHAPTER 20

"That was me," William Foxwell said. Or I dreamed that was what he said. My eyes were shut, I was facedown on my pillow, and I was dead asleep.

"Hunh?" I said into my pillow, trying to force myself up but too tired at first to do it.

"The machine gunner," William Foxwell said. "The one who was late getting to the torpedo plane. The one Dewey saw as he was heading for his battle station. That was me."

I managed to push myself free of the pillow and lift my head, though not enough yet to see to the end of the bed where William Foxwell customarily sat when he visited. I hadn't gotten very far back into the Midway book before I fell asleep earlier. It was still lying on the bed next to me.

Meanwhile, what William Foxwell had just said, or what I thought he'd just said, hardly made any sense. I shook my head to try to clear it some more. He wasn't on any of the flight crews, and he sure wasn't a machine gunner — that much I knew for sure.

"Where have you been?" I asked.

"Nearby," he said. "Some of the time, anyway. It sort of felt too hard for a while there to get to you guys. Not that I didn't try."

I didn't understand that, either, but let it go.

"Did I hear you right?" I asked. "Did you say you were on one of the torpedo bombers during the Battle of Midway?" I sat up the rest of the way and leaned against the headboard on my bed. I didn't think I could hold my head up without some help. "Is that what you said?" I asked again.

"I'm pretty sure so," William Foxwell said, though his voice was already starting to sound funny, far away one minute, closer the next. "It's what came back to me when you all were talking to Dewey."

"Were you there when we were on the phone with him?"

I asked. "At Uncle Dex's? Because none of us saw you or anything."

"Sort of yes and sort of no," he answered. "It's hard to explain. But I did hear some of the conversation."

"And that helped you remember that you were on one of the torpedo planes?" I asked. "But how?"

"Thought you'd be interested in that," William Foxwell said, pressing his hands down on my mattress, not that it did anything. "Believe me, I was very interested in that myself. It was when I went down to the head, like Dewey said."

"About that," I interrupted. "I meant to ask Dewey — Mr. Tomzak — but what's the 'head'?"

"Toilet," William Foxwell replied. "I had — well, most of us on ship had, at one time or another — what they used to call the runs."

"I think I can figure that one out," I said, making a face.

"Anyway," he continued, "I was coming back up the metal stairs, hurrying back to where I was supposed to be. Wasn't anybody else around except a guy I recognized from one of the flight crews. He was carrying his flight suit, rushing to get to the same place I was just coming from and he slipped and fell and hit his head. He was pretty loopy. I guess you could say he didn't know what day it was or anything like that. Probably had a concussion.

"Meanwhile, they were barking orders on the loudspeakers all over the ship, and the main order was for flight crews to report to the flight deck and prepare for takeoff. But there was no way this guy was making it to his plane. I already knew they were bringing up the torpedo bombers, the Devastators, which was a plane I knew inside and out, and in just that split second I saw that this was my chance to make up for what I did, or what I didn't do, in the Battle of the Coral Sea."

"You pretended you were him?" I asked, incredulous.

"There still wasn't anybody else around in that one part of the ship," he said, not answering me directly. "I didn't have time to go for help. So I made sure the guy that hit his head was propped up okay where somebody could find him. Then I grabbed his flight suit and pulled it on over my uniform. They were still yelling all over the ship for the torpedo bomber crews and I ran up to the flight deck, jamming the headgear on right when I got there."

"How did you know which plane to get on?" I asked.

William Foxwell nodded his serious nod. "I just looked for the one in need of a machine gunner," he said.

"Didn't anybody realize you weren't the right guy?"

"Nope," he said. "I did see Dewey on the other side of the flight deck, heading below, probably to a fireman's station. My Devastator was already taxiing into position for takeoff, so I ran over and they boosted me up and nobody asked me a thing. As soon as I buckled in, I realized I hadn't grabbed the gunner's parachute, and I just about climbed back down to go find it, but it was too late. We jerked forward in the takeoff line and that was that. I wrapped my fingers around the double-barrel machine guns they had back there, just to get the feel of them. I already knew how to shoot — I'd figured that out those countless times I'd checked out the planes whenever our cleaning crew was on the flight deck. But knowing and doing, those are two very different things, let me tell you."

I was straining to follow all that William Foxwell was saying. It was two in the morning and I was still feeling fuzzy from being woken up from a deep sleep, and he also kept doing that fading in and out thing with his voice, as if it was a struggle for him to keep the volume up loud enough for me to hear.

He kept talking, and after a while it seemed as if he was talking as much to himself as to me.

"Next thing I knew we were flying, climbing high enough to stay with the squad formation to try to locate the

Japanese fleet. We'd heard back on ship that they had already launched the torpedo planes from the *Enterprise* and the *Hornet* first, before us. The *Yorktown* Devastators would be the last ones, coming in to finish off the job. I guess. Only when we found the Japanese ships, it didn't look like any of them had been hit at all. What we did see were a lot of our planes in the water, burning, blasted to pieces."

I realized I knew part of the story — maybe a lot of it — that William Foxwell didn't, even though he'd been there. "I don't know if you heard us talking about it before," I said, "but none of the torpedo bombers hit their targets. They almost all got shot down." I felt awful being the one to tell him, but he had to know.

William nodded sadly. "Well, we tried," he said. "But one minute we were flying along, just spotting the Imperial Navy and their aircraft carriers, and the next minute we were getting shot at from behind. I rotated in the rear cockpit and saw three Zeroes were already on us. One shot up a wing, but we managed to keep going. Another hit the cockpit and I was pretty sure wounded the pilot, but he kept us flying, taking us down lower toward the water. We had to get down there, just above the waves, to line up and fire that thousand-pound torpedo that was weighing us down."

"Did you shoot back at them?" I asked, caught up in the story — as awful as it was.

"Yeah," he said. "I did. Or I tried. They were so fast, though! Like buzzing bees or something. Every time I opened up, they disappeared, and then they reappeared somewhere else, shooting at us from another angle. All that saved us was going so low over the ocean that the Zeroes couldn't maneuver around us and had to give up."

"What happened then?" I asked, all my weariness totally gone. I was practically hyperventilating, wanting to know.

"Everything and nothing," William Foxwell said, sounding glum all of a sudden. "The torpedo released too soon. Didn't even explode. Just must have sunk."

"Oh no!" I said loudly.

"I couldn't believe it," he said.

"Then what?" I asked, quieter this time, with a bad feeling.

"Then they killed the pilot," he said. "I saw him slump over. At first, we kept flying straight, low over the water. I emptied the last of the rounds from the machine gun at one of the Japanese carriers, not that I was even in range. And then we went down."

I let the silence between us just sit there for a minute, before I asked the question.

"So was that where everything, you know, ended?" I asked.

The silence came back — such a deep silence that I could hear myself breathing, almost panting as I waited for William Foxwell to break it.

"No," he finally said. "I don't think so. It's kind of a blur — the plane hitting the water and spinning like crazy. No way the bombardier could have survived the impact. And then the nose of the plane going under. Me climbing out of my shoulder harness to see if I could help the pilot, even though I already knew it was too late for him. It seemed like just seconds, though, before the cockpit submerged with his body still trapped in it. I climbed out on a wing, but then even that went under, and then the rest of the plane, too.

"Gone," he said. "And me treading water in the middle of the Pacific Ocean while the battle still went on all around me. Surrounded by Japanese ships. Grabbing whatever I could find to stay afloat."

"Just like George Gay!" I exclaimed.

"Who?" William Foxwell asked.

"He was a torpedo bomber pilot, too, but I think he was on the *Hornet*. He was the only one in his squad who survived. He hid under a seat cushion after his plane went down so the Japanese wouldn't find him, all day and all night. A seaplane finally rescued him the next day. He wrote a book about it after the war. He got pretty famous."

William Foxwell nodded. "That's good news he got rescued. Didn't know him or know anything about that. About all I did know at the time was how hard it was getting to keep my head above water, and how scared I was of both sharks and the Japanese. I was pretty sure my leg was broken, down at my ankle, from the crash landing into the ocean. But I couldn't think about that too much. Everything was happening so fast all around me."

He hesitated. "I remember thinking everything was lost," he said. "Not just the planes and everybody flying them on our side, but the whole battle. Maybe even the war."

He wrinkled his brow, going even deeper into his thoughts or memory or whatever. "And then . . . ," he started, and stopped.

"And then what?" I asked, desperate to hear.

"And then everything changed." His face brightened.

"How?" I asked. "What?" I really, really wished I'd finished reading my book about the Battle of Midway so I'd already know this stuff.

"Dive-bombers," he said. "It was our dive-bombers on the attack. Coming straight down at the Japanese carriers, right out of the sun. Turned out we weren't done just quite yet!"

CHAPTER 21

"I remember struggling to keep my head above water in the ocean," William Foxwell was saying. It was now so deep in the night I didn't want to look at the clock and see how much sleep I wasn't going to get, or how soon before I'd have to get up for school.

"I also remember being so close to the Japanese ships that I was afraid if one of them turned my way I'd get run over and drowned," he said. "All I had to help me was a half-inflated life vest. Not even half inflated, really. Just barely enough air in it so I could hang on."

"Was that when the dive-bombers attacked?" I asked.

"Not yet," he said. "First what I saw was all the Japanese

planes landing back on their four giant aircraft carriers to refuel. Not just the Zeroes that had shot down all our torpedo bombers, but a lot of their bombers, too."

"I bet those were the ones that had attacked Midway," I said.

William Foxwell shrugged. "Maybe so. I didn't have any way to know, but that could well be. So that's when I was at my lowest. All our torpedo bombers shot down, no damage to any of the Japanese ships. My plane gone down to the bottom, with the poor pilot and bombardier. And me a sitting duck with that half of a life vest in the middle of the ocean, nowhere to run and nowhere to hide. And I guessed the Japanese planes were refueling to go attack our ships, which they must have found by then with their scout planes."

"And *that's* when our dive-bombers attacked?" I asked again.

William Foxwell smiled, but it was a half-sad smile. "Yeah. That's when it happened. The Japanese hadn't counted on those dive-bombers, and they hadn't seen them, either. Apparently, the divers were flying so high coming in from the *Yorktown* and the *Hornet* and the *Enterprise* that the Japanese didn't have time to send their Zeroes out to meet them, and shoot them down, too. There was cloud cover, and they were coming out of the sun. The Japanese almost didn't know what hit them."

He shook his head, I guess picturing it again in his mind, and then he continued.

"All the antiaircraft guns started firing away," he said. "I could feel it in the water. Shook up everything. Felt like it rattled my bones, and made that broken leg hurt something awful." He reached down to rub his ankle, as if that old pain was somehow still there, even though he was a ghost now and I was pretty sure ghosts couldn't feel pain. At least not the physical kind.

William Foxwell's voice got softer, fainter again. "I guess every one of those Japanese planes must have refueled already because when the dive-bombers dropped their bombs, it seemed like every one I saw was a direct hit on the carriers, and every explosion let loose a firestorm from all those planes exploding with all that fuel." He shook his head again, practically whispering now. "And one fire would start another, and then another, and then another until it spread to almost everywhere, even the water around the ships where the fuel spilled and spread. The dive-bombers kept coming and their bombs kept hitting the flight decks of those carriers. The whole ships seemed to be on fire. And then there were the secondary explosions as the fires spread to the engine rooms and the munitions."

I was practically bouncing on my bed with excitement,

hearing this part of the story. The good guys were finally winning!

He paused again. His face darkened. "It felt good at first. All that destruction thanks to the dive-bombers — it was revenge for all our boys who'd been shot down, and meant that the torpedo bomber crews hadn't died in vain, you know? It was like the Devastators were the decoys, only nobody thought about it that way at the time. But that's what they — I guess *we* — were. Once the Japanese shot all of us out of the sky, and none of our bombs hit, they let their guard down; that's when the dive-bombers came in and surprised them. Caught them with their pants down, so to speak. I was happy, too, because it looked like us taking out all their carriers — it would turn the tide of the battle our way.

"But then I remembered our own boys on the *Yorktown* when that armor-piercing bomb hit us at Coral Sea, and I knew the same thing was happening to their boys — the Japanese sailors. All of them just doing their jobs, following their orders, hoping to survive the war and go back home to their families.

"Only that wouldn't be happening for so many of them. Thousands, I bet." He sighed. "And it wouldn't be happening for me, either."

"Are you okay?" I asked. His voice was trembling. I felt bad for him, and bad for all of them — all those brave Americans who were killed, and now the Japanese sailors, too.

He shrugged, and then faded quickly — faster than before. His voice came from so far away that I could barely hear him.

"William!" I said, panicked. Was this it? Was this the last time I'd see him? I'd never seen him like this before.

"Can't remember exactly what happened next," he said, just before vanishing altogether. "Only thing that I'm about half sure of is that I didn't drown the way I was afraid would happen, and no shark got me, either. I have this picture of me, dripping wet, standing on my bum leg, and somebody talking to me — in Japanese."

I stared at the empty space at the foot of my bed. Was it too late to save him?

·   ·   ·

I sat there for quite a while after he disappeared, not moving, not doing anything except think about everything William Foxwell had just told me. It was four in the morning and I knew I would never get back to sleep. So I finally roused myself and did the only logical thing at that time of the night that there was left to do after everything I'd just heard from William Foxwell. I picked up my Midway book, found the place I'd left off before, and started reading again. We had to keep trying.

The account in my book laid things out pretty much the way William Foxwell had described them: the dive-bombers raining bombs down on the Japanese carriers, destroying three of the four that day, and the fourth one in another attack later on.

Meanwhile, a Japanese scout plane had finally discovered the location of one of the American aircraft carriers. It was William Foxwell's ship, the *Yorktown*. The Japanese still had that fourth carrier at the time, and so sent their remaining bombers out on the attack. The *Yorktown* took several direct hits and nearly sank. Hundreds of the men on board were killed. The rest had to abandon ship.

But doomed ship or not, the *Yorktown* still wouldn't go down the way everybody expected, though it was a sitting duck, barely able to move, even with the help of other ships. The *Yorktown* was slowly crawling back toward the Hawaiian Islands the next day when the end finally came. A Japanese submarine found, and torpedoed, the *Yorktown* and an escort ship, blasting the escort ship literally in two, and sinking the *Yorktown*.

As I read the chapter, I realized that William Foxwell

didn't know anything about that, and I wondered if I should tell him — and if I'd even have the opportunity. How hard would that be, to find out that even more of his friends had been killed in the Battle of Midway, all those guys he and Dewey Tomzak had served with for months and months at sea? I wasn't so sure he needed to know that. Maybe he hadn't heard what Mr. Tomzak told us about the *Yorktown* being a doomed ship. He hadn't brought it up, anyway, and so I decided the next time I saw William I wouldn't bring it up, either. I just hoped that there would be a next time.

·　·　·

The battle still wasn't over even then, with the sinking of the *Yorktown*. The U.S. retaliated by sending the last of their bombers from their other two carriers, the *Hornet* and the *Enterprise*, to find and sink that last Japanese aircraft carrier, and with it any chance the Japanese had of taking Midway, and Hawaii, and attacking California.

I sped through the next chapter in the book to learn what happened and found the two words I was looking for — and that marked the end of the Battle of Midway:

"Mission accomplished."

But what did that mean for William?

Once again I didn't have a chance to fill Greg and Julie in on any of this until lunchtime. That didn't work out too well, either. I had just started telling them about William Foxwell and the rear cockpit gunner and the accident belowdecks outside the head when a shadow darkened our table.

We all looked up, surprised. Of course, it was Belman.

"Hello, dorks," he said.

Julie stiffened. Greg grabbed the edges of his tray — as if he was going to actually hit the guy with it this time. I scooted my chair back as far as it would go, which unfortunately wasn't very far because of the wall.

"What do you want?" Julie demanded.

"Oh, nothing," he said in this phony sweet voice. "Just came by to say hi. Oh yeah, and to tell you I'm looking forward to seeing you three at the All-Ages Open Mic Night. My band's playing. Yeah, that's right. I have a band, too, only it's a real band and not a wizard dork band."

"We're not a wizard band," Greg said indignantly. "Not that there's anything wrong with that if we were."

"Hey," Belman said, "Wrock and Rowling! Isn't that what you dorks like to say?" He pointed at me and said, "Harry." Then he pointed at Greg and said, "Ron."

He pointed at Julie next, but she beat him to it.

"Hermione," she said. "And 'loseriest' isn't even a word, by the way. *And* those wizard bands play some great music. You should check them out on YouTube some time." Then she stomped on his foot.

We got out of there fast.

· · ·

"Do you think he's going to do something to us?" I asked, once we were safe out of the cafeteria and hiding in a narrow, unused hallway in the math wing. "I mean, he said he has a band."

"I hope he does," Greg said, brandishing an empty lunch

tray, which he'd carried with him for some reason. "I've got this tray, and I'm not afraid to use it."

Julie let go of one of her rare smiles. "He was probably in too much pain. But never mind him. We'll deal with him later. Anderson, you have to tell us what the ghost said last night. Quickly."

"The ghost has a name, remember?" I said. "It's William — William Foxwell."

"Yes, of course," Julie said, rolling her eyes. "So tell us."

I gave as quick a summary as I could — about William Foxwell helping the rear cockpit gunner after he hit his head, about William putting on the flight suit and climbing on the Devastator, about the takeoff and locating the Japanese fleet, about the Zeroes and the plane crash into the ocean. I told them all the rest of it, too — everything else I had read about the Battle of Midway, including what happened to the *Yorktown* later on.

Greg jumped in when I finished. "You're not going to believe this," he said, "but I stayed up really late last night, too, and I was exploring on the Internet."

"Why wouldn't we believe that?" I asked, annoyed that he was changing the subject. "Were you watching your favorite funny animal videos on YouTube?"

Greg scowled at me. "No," he said. "I found these discussion groups for guys that had fought in the war, and for their family members who had questions about what happened to their grandfathers or whatever. I spent a lot of time just scrolling through the ones from World War II. You could look up what they had to say about different battles, so I went to the Battle of Midway."

"Good work, Greg," I said, feeling kind of bad and trying to make up for what I'd said.

"Thanks," he said. "Anyway, I came across this one post; it was from a guy who said his grandfather had told him the strangest story years ago, about how the grandfather was supposed to be on one of the torpedo bombers at Midway only he had an accident and hit his head and never made it to his plane."

"That must have been the guy!" I shouted. "The rear cockpit gunner whose place William Foxwell took!"

"Yeah," Greg continued, grinning. "The grandfather had told his grandson that when he regained consciousness his flight suit was gone, and all the planes had already taken off. But the guys he talked to on the flight deck all insisted that there were pilots and rear cockpit gunners and bombardiers on all of them, so he didn't know what to think. He decided that either everybody was confused, or else there was a rear cockpit gunner ghost that took his place. They weren't ever able to solve the mystery — everybody on board was too busy sending out the dive-bombers after the torpedo bombers were all gone, and then they got attacked later on by the Japanese, and then I guess they got sunk and a lot of the sailors lost their lives and the rest had to abandon ship."

Julie had already pulled out a notebook and pencil. "What's the name of the site?" she said. "I'll look it up, and we'll find the grandfather and ask him more about what happened."

"Can't," Greg said. "The guy who posted the story said his grandfather died ten years ago."

"Did anybody else comment on the post?" Julie asked.

Greg shook his head. "I guess so many of the guys who were in the service back then, they're really old now — in their nineties. Not too many of them are left."

I couldn't help thinking about my great-grandpa just then. He was Pop Pop's dad and he died before I was born. He'd been in the war, too, in a way — working in a factory that made tanks and armored cars and army trucks and stuff. Pop Pop told me about him. I guess it was a time when everybody pitched in together in whatever way they could. It was sad to think of them all being so old now, and passing away. It made me kind of proud, too, though — that they had done all that for us.

The bell rang and Julie put away her notebook.

"At least what Greg found out confirms William Foxwell's story," I said. "That what he said happened must have really happened."

"But what about the last thing he told you?" Greg asked as we pushed ourselves out into the stream of kids pouring down the hall. "About somebody speaking to him in Japanese?"

"Maybe he got captured by the Japanese," I said. "Maybe they rescued him. It's the only thing that makes sense."

"There *were* some men of the flight crews who survived their crash landing and who were captured," Julie said, though she wasn't smiling.

"That must have been it, then," I said. "He was captured."

Greg chimed in after me. "So maybe he lived a lot longer than the war," he said hopefully. "Like, they just kept him prisoner while the war was going on. Maybe he tried to escape."

Julie shook her head. "No," she said. "I read about this in the book I assigned to myself. They brought the prisoners on board Japanese ships and interrogated them. In one of the accounts I read, they threatened the American pilot with a sword. The Japanese demanded the men tell them the position of the American ships. Especially the aircraft carriers."

"And then what?" I asked, though I had that sinking feeling again about what she was going to say next.

"They were executed," she said. "Their bodies were returned to the ocean."

"Oh no," I said.

Greg was outraged. "Wasn't that against the law? Weren't they supposed to just keep them in a prison camp or something?"

"You're thinking about the Geneva Conventions," I said. Pop Pop had told me all about them. "Those are the international laws about the treatment of prisoners — that you aren't supposed to execute a prisoner unless he is a spy. You're supposed to treat prisoners humanely."

"Then it *was* against the law," Greg said.

"Yes, I would suppose so," Julie said. "But in war, apparently, everyone doesn't follow the law. But in any case there is another problem."

"Which is what?" I asked. We were standing in the middle of the hall, so caught up in the conversation that we hadn't split up to go to our separate classes. But I didn't say anything. I had to know the rest — about this other problem.

"It's about the names I found in my book," she said. "The names of the prisoners."

She looked up at the ceiling for a minute, then continued. "None of them was William Foxwell."

CHAPTER 23

Band practice went surprisingly well that afternoon. We figured we needed three songs for the All-Ages Open Mic Night, so Julie led us through another one she had written. It was called "Hamster Talks," and it was a hamster talking about how much it sucked to be in a cage all day, but also how great it was when little kids took you out and played with you, and how cool it was that you could go to the bathroom anywhere and your humans had to clean it up, and then still had to feed you every day whether they wanted to or not, and give you plenty of water. It was kind of hilarious.

"So you have a hamster?" Greg asked her, obviously expecting her to say yes.

"No," Julie said. "They're disgusting."

Greg and I were both confused. "Then why did you write the song," I asked, "if you hate hamsters?"

Julie insisted that she didn't hate hamsters, she just found them disgusting, like she'd said, and anyway, what was wrong with writing a song about a hamster?

It was actually a pretty catchy tune, and helped us take our minds off what might have happened to William Foxwell, and how he could have heard a Japanese voice after he crash-landed in the Pacific during the Battle of Midway.

.   .   .

Julie called me that night just as I was crawling into bed. I was running on fumes, as Dad likes to say when he's super tired and hasn't had enough sleep in a while. I'd been up practically the whole night before, so I was feeling about half dead myself.

"I'm worried about William Foxwell," Julie said, doing her usual thing of skipping over the hello part of the phone call. "And I'm sorry that I called him 'the ghost' this afternoon."

"That's okay," I said. "I guess it's easy to forget sometimes that he's human. Or that he used to be."

"We need him to come back again soon," Julie said. "So we can ask him for more that he can remember about the

· 165 ·

Japanese voice. He has to help us help him. You have to summon him, or whatever it is you do."

"But that's just the problem, Julie," I said, feeling helpless. "I can't summon him. He just shows up whenever he wants to. Or whenever he can. And he told me that it seems to be getting harder sometimes."

"He didn't come tonight?" she asked.

"No," I said. "Not so far. Sometimes when I give up wondering if he will, like if I just fall asleep, or get busy doing homework or whatever, then he might show up."

"Then fall asleep right now," Julie ordered. "I'll hang up and perhaps he'll come when you are sleeping and you can ask him."

I couldn't tell if she was joking or not. "Ask him what exactly?" I asked.

"If there was a prisoner that no one knew about, that wasn't in any of the records of the Japanese or the Americans or anyone. And if he was that secret prisoner of the Battle of Midway."

•   •   •

It's hard to fall asleep when you're trying to, especially if you're trying as hard as I was that night, and if you're as worried as I was that we might not be able to solve the mystery of William Foxwell in time, but somehow I managed.

As soon as I fell asleep I had another dream about him. Once again, like in the last dream I had about William Foxwell, I was on a boat in the ocean, only this time I found him. He was treading water, exhausted, struggling to keep his head up. I extended my arm as far out of the boat as I could, but every time he reached up to grab my hand, he slipped under the waves and had to use both hands to pull himself back up and keep from drowning. I didn't see a life vest, or half a life vest, or anything that might keep him from drowning. It was just me and him. Greg wasn't even there this time. This went on for a long time, me reaching and never quite getting to him, and William slipping under. And then there was a shadow over both of us. I heard shouting — in Japanese. I looked up and it was some kind of Japanese ship. All the Japanese sailors and officers were angry, and yelling at us, barking orders that we couldn't understand.

I looked back to see what was happening with William Foxwell, to try one last time to pull him into my boat so we could try to escape — but he wasn't there.

* * *

For the next three days in real life, I waited for him to come see me. At school I was so distracted that I messed up on a couple of tests and forgot to turn in three assignments, and so got hammered with a ton of extra homework. Not to mention how mad at me Mom and Dad were because I was doing so poorly in school.

"You're a smart kid!" Mom kept saying. "So do the work already!"

Dad threatened to break up the band and not let us practice anymore after school — or participate in the All-Ages Open Mic Night, which was in just two more weeks.

Our band practices were pretty flat. Julie used the word "desultory," which Greg and I had to look up. It means "disconnected" and "lacking in consistency," which totally fit. Nobody said it, but I was sure we were all afraid of the same thing: that we had taken too long finding the answers we needed for William Foxwell, and now it was too late.

Greg actually seemed to be taking it the hardest of everybody. It was like he was genuinely depressed, like William Foxwell had been his own dad or brother or uncle or something. I thought he was even going to start crying one day at practice when Julie asked me if there was anything new — any middle-of-the-night visits, any information — and I said no. That was on the third day of no William Foxwell.

And then, out of desperation, I guess, Julie came up with

a crazy idea that seemed like about the longest of long shots that I could imagine.

. . .

"I told my dad about our problem," Julie said to Greg and me at lunch. "Not everything, of course. I explained that this was Anderson's relative, and we were searching for the answer to his disappearance in the war. I told my dad that it was important to Anderson and to his family, and I asked if he had any suggestions for us in our quest to solve the mystery."

"And did he?" Greg asked.

Julie nodded emphatically. "Yes. After I explained about our theory — that perhaps there was a fourth pilot or someone from one of the U.S. torpedo bomber flight crews who was captured by the Japanese — my dad said that my great-great-uncle had served in the Imperial Navy during the war."

"Is he still alive?" I asked.

"He is," Julie said.

"Wait, was your great-great-uncle on one of the Japanese ships at Midway?" Greg asked eagerly.

Suddenly, we were both excited.

But Julie shook her head. "Great-Great Uncle was still only in training at that time, so early in the war."

Greg tapped his spoon in a pile of instant mashed potatoes

on his lunch tray, leaving little craters. "Well, so much for that," he said.

I wasn't so ready to give up. "Maybe you could call him?" I suggested. "See if he knows anything, or knows somebody who might know. I mean, it's not as if we have a whole lot of other options — or ideas."

"Yeah," Greg chimed in. "Good point. I guess." He didn't sound at all enthusiastic.

Julie was, though.

"I already called him," she announced.

"Your great-great-uncle?" I asked.

"Yes," she said. "Last night. Which was his morning, of course, in Japan."

"Well, don't keep us in suspense," Greg said. "What did he say?"

Julie smiled one of those actual smiles of hers. "He said that he did have a friend, who was a very young officer at the time, who served on a destroyer for the Imperial Navy, and it was one of the escort ships for the Japanese carrier fleet that attacked the island of Midway. Great-Great-Uncle said that he would call his friend and talk to him, to see if he had ever heard anything about a mysterious fourth American captured after all the planes were shot out of the sky."

Greg shoveled in a mouthful of potatoes. I took a bite of my soggy sandwich.

After he swallowed, Greg asked when Julie thought we'd hear back from Great-Great-Uncle's friend. Julie shrugged. She was eating shiny peas from green pods out of a plastic container that she'd brought from home. She said it was called edamame, and it was Japanese.

"Hopefully, we hear something soon, but these men — Great-Great-Uncle and his friend — are very old and do not move quickly. I only hope Great-Great-Uncle remembers his promise to call. Until then, we wait," Julie said.

"I hope it's soon enough," Greg said. "And I hope he knows something that can help. I don't think we have much time."

. . .

We had another good band practice that afternoon — even when Uncle Dex came down with his electric ukulele to sit in on "How Can I Miss You When You Won't Go Away?" — which I was having my doubts about us performing. I still wasn't sold on Julie's "Hamster Talks," either, but she seemed to have established herself as the band leader, and it was obvious that Greg was fine with it, no matter what I might think.

It was pretty ironic, too, us singing "How Can I Miss

You When You Won't Go Away?" when I was sitting there missing William Foxwell, and hoping he hadn't gone away, or at least not totally away. Not yet. Not until we had the answers he needed.

My mind must have wandered, thinking about all that stuff, because Julie stopped playing and got on me about messing up the chords.

"Pay attention, Anderson," she said. "We'll never win if we don't get this right."

"Wait," I said, caught off guard. "Win what? I thought we were just playing the open mic night. Us and everybody else who has a middle school band. Including Belman."

"Yeah," Greg said. "That's right. But it's also a competition. Didn't you see the flyers they posted around school? Like, the fine print? Whoever they vote the winner gets to do a whole concert at Halloween."

I hadn't read the fine print, of course. I'd been distracted worrying about William Foxwell. But now that they said it, I was suddenly nervous, and when we went through it again I messed up even more. And this time I *was* paying attention.

• • •

It was hard waiting to hear back from Great-Great-Uncle. The longer it took, the more discouraged I felt. Mom noticed that I was dragging around at the end of the second day of waiting and asked me what was going on. I couldn't exactly tell her, of course, and that was hard, too. I always used to tell Mom everything, but even before William Foxwell came into my life, I had stopped. After her diagnosis, and when she started having such a hard time with the MS, I didn't want to add anything else to all that she had to worry about. So if it was anything bad or sad, I either told Dad or kept it to myself.

"I've just been trying to help this guy, sort of this friend of mine," I said. "But sometimes I guess you can't just fix things for somebody no matter how much you want to."

I figured being vague like that would be okay, and it was. Mom pulled me down on the couch next to her and gave me a hug. "Well, I'm sure it means a lot to your friend that you're trying to help," she said. "And just that you care, and your friend knows you care — I'm betting that can lift his spirits, too."

Mom seemed happy to be giving me advice and all, and that made me happy, too. I hoped she was right, that it *did* help William Foxwell to somehow know how hard we were working to get the answers he needed and everything — and that we did care so much. Even if we hadn't seen him in nearly a week.

I thanked Mom and went to my bedroom. Just before I went to sleep I whispered aloud everything that had been going on, on the chance that William Foxwell was nearby and able to hear me, even if he was stuck on the other side of some sort of invisible curtain in a place where I couldn't hear him back.

That night I had yet another dream about William. Everything was fuzzy at first, but then as it slowly came into focus, I realized we were both on a Japanese ship — which from what I could tell, after looking at so many pictures of ships while reading about the Battle of Midway — was one of the escort boats, a destroyer.

William Foxwell was kneeling on the deck, surrounded by Imperial Navy officers. They were shouting at him. I could see it all but couldn't speak, couldn't move, couldn't do anything. It was as if I was the ghost and he was real, and alive.

He lifted his head in the dream and looked past the officers at me, and he said just one word: "This."

"This what?" I tried to say back, only my voice still didn't work. "Are you trying to tell me this is what happened to you?"

He couldn't answer, and everything went out of focus again. But somehow I knew that he was reaching out to me in the dream, and that, as he continued to fade away from me and from Julie and Greg and everything, this was as close as he could get.

CHAPTER 24

We were at band practice the next day when Julie got the call. Greg and I pressed in as close as we could to hear the conversation, even though it was all in Japanese, and even though Julie had to apologize and tell Great-Great-Uncle the reception was bad and she had to go upstairs. We followed her out of the dank basement and up past Uncle Dex and out onto the sidewalk, practically shaking with excitement.

But then, as they talked, Julie's face fell and I knew it was bad news. Greg saw it, too. He punched the Kitchen Sink door and scraped up his hand.

"I'm sorry," Julie said when she got off the phone.

"Great-Great-Uncle says his friend, Mr. Yamaguchi, remembers nothing. No American prisoner of war was picked up in the Pacific Ocean by the destroyer; there's nothing to tell. Mr. Yamaguchi asked Great-Great-Uncle to not contact him again. He was angry that Great-Great-Uncle invaded his privacy, and adamant that we are to leave him alone."

Julie and Greg both teared up. I might have, too. "Great-Great-Uncle says he's sorry for disappointing us," Julie said. "He says it is so difficult for those who served, even so many years later, to talk about the war."

We stood there for a while, not talking, nobody moving, until finally we filed silently back inside.

"Why the long faces?" Uncle Dex asked. "Something the matter?"

Greg and Julie didn't say anything, so it fell on me to answer. "It's just this friend of ours who we were trying to help," I said, which was pretty much the same thing I had said to Mom the night before.

Thankfully, Uncle Dex didn't ask anything else.

Nobody was in the mood for rehearsing, but nobody was in the mood for going home, either, I guess. I know I wasn't. It was hard enough knowing we'd let down William Foxwell without being all alone, too.

We were all just sitting there, messing around with our instruments because we didn't know what else to do, but not really playing or anything. And that's when he came back, the very faint outline of him, anyway.

When he spoke, his voice sounded so far away that it was practically like he was trying to talk to us from seventy years ago.

"I just wanted to thank you," we heard him say. "For all you've done. It was so great of you and I know you did your best. And, hey, I even got to play the trumpet again, so that was something good that came out of it all, too, even if I was a little, uh, rusty."

I couldn't believe it. William Foxwell was actually trying to be cheerful, or at least not distraught, which was how we were all feeling, all the way down to our bones. I couldn't believe it was going to end this way, after we had come so close. And now he was doomed to that limbo or wherever it was he'd been wandering and lost all these years.

"It was an honor knowing the three of you," he said, his voice even fainter than before. And then the outline, the faraway voice, everything about William Foxwell blinked out like the last ember of a fire. It was almost as if he'd never been here at all.

· · ·

You'd think at least one good thing would have happened after that — like us winning the All-Ages Open Mic Night Competition and getting a standing ovation, and everybody in school knowing our names and deciding we were these three quirky but also very cool kids.

But it didn't happen quite that way.

First, Greg's dad hit another rough patch and got mad at him for not cleaning up his room and grounded him. That didn't stop Greg from sneaking out, of course, but it did make him really late for the concert. He called to tell us what happened and that he was on his way.

Julie and I were nervously waiting for him, standing right next to the stage with our instruments, when Belman and his band got up to perform. They were playing right before us. Belman's band was called the Bass Rats, which I had to admit was a pretty good name.

First, he introduced himself and his bandmates, and then he thanked everybody for coming out to hear them and said he looked forward to winning the competition. Everybody except Julie and me laughed.

"He's so conceited," Julie said.

Unfortunately, he was also really good and everybody rocked out to all of the Bass Rats' songs.

There were about fifty kids in the audience, mostly middle school and high school kids, though a few looked as if they might still be in elementary school. All the parents, my dad included, were sitting in a sort of parents' waiting room out in the front of this long warehouse that was a drum studio/ alternative music concert venue called Eyeclops. Their logo was a giant eye in the middle of a pyramid. I wasn't sure what that had to do with drums. It looked more like what you see on a dollar bill.

"Thank you, everybody," Belman yelled into the mic after their last song. "It's great to be here in Fredericksburg!"

Julie sniffed. "He says that as if his band has ever played anywhere else," she said.

Belman wasn't finished. "I want you guys to be really nice to the next band up." He gestured toward us, where we were waiting in the wings. "They're all in third grade, and I'm pretty sure it's the first time they've been away from their mommies. This might also be a good time to take a break if you want. Maybe go outside and get some fresh air because, I mean, they're just learning how to play, so it could get really ugly in here."

Every one of those fifty kids — including the real elementaries — looked at me and Julie and laughed when Belman said that. And dumb me, I couldn't help myself. I yelled out, "We're not in third grade!" But that just made people laugh more.

"Of course you're not," Belman said, with that big, weird grin of his.

Julie and I just stood there and fumed. What else could we do?

At that moment Greg finally showed up, but everything went even more downhill after that. We went onstage after the Bass Rats left, but we couldn't get our instruments tuned right. Julie got frustrated and snapped at us, which only made people laugh some more. Once we started, Greg tried singing louder to make up for it, but he was off-key or something and his voice kept breaking in the middle of certain notes. A *lot* of certain notes.

It was a disaster, and I couldn't wait for it to be over. We only did two of our three songs because I wasn't about to let Greg and his cracking voice start singing about hamsters, no matter who wrote the lyrics. Nobody called for an encore, which was fine with me. I practically ran offstage when we finished, and wished I could keep running — out the door, out of the building, all the way home to try to convince Mom and Dad that we should move to a different town where nobody had ever heard of me before.

CHAPTER 25

Afterward, Greg tried to convince us, and himself, that it wasn't that bad. "Really, once I got warmed up, I thought it sounded fine. And I bet nobody even noticed we weren't in tune."

"It was my fault," I said to try and make him feel better. "I kept forgetting the chords."

"Oh, stop it, you two," Julie finally said. "We just need more practice. We were distracted. We have to rededicate ourselves to our mission."

I rolled my eyes. "We have to rededicate ourselves to being invisible at school," I said. "People are going to be making fun of us from now until we graduate. From high school! I mean, what were we thinking? And I'm pretty sure Belman and his band will win."

"Doesn't seem fair," Greg said. "He's such a jerk and all."

"Yes," Julie said. "Where's the poetic justice?"

"What's that?" Greg asked.

I answered. "It's when the good guys win and the bad guys get what's coming to them — their just deserts."

"Just deserts?" Greg repeated.

Julie sighed. "They get punished," she said.

"Oh," Greg said. "Well, that sure didn't happen tonight. Or with anything, lately."

"You mean with William Foxwell?" I asked.

He didn't have to answer. We all knew what he was talking about.

We were standing on the sidewalk in front of the Eyeclops studio having our conversation, and after a while, Dad came out to find us. "You guys ready to go?" he asked.

"Just in a minute, Dad," I said. "We have to go back inside and get our instruments."

Dad said he would wait in the parents' room, and for us to come get him when we were ready.

None of us was in a hurry to get laughed at some more, so we just stood there, listening to the strains of what sounded like dying cats back inside Eyeclops. I figured it must be that band with the actual elementary kids. At least there was somebody worse than us. Not that that made me feel any better.

And then Julie's phone rang.

She fished it out of the pocket in her cargo pants, and said, "Huh."

"Huh, what?" Greg asked.

"Huh, it's from Japan."

"Well, answer it already," I said, and so she did.

Her jaw dropped almost immediately after she said hello. She covered the speaker, looked at us, blinked three times, and said, "It's Mr. Yamaguchi!"

"Great-Great-Uncle's friend?" Greg said.

Julie nodded, already speaking Japanese again over the phone.

I felt a weird chill for a second and found myself looking around, expecting to see William Foxwell.

Julie paused in her conversation to translate for us. "Mr. Yamaguchi asks us to please forgive him for being impolite."

And then, a minute later: "Mr. Yamaguchi says Great-Great-Uncle gave him my telephone number, and he insisted on calling us himself instead of sending a message through Great-Great-Uncle."

And another minute later: "He says he must tell us a truth he has kept hidden all these years. He says he was a young naval officer on the destroyer, searching for Japanese survivors from one of the Japanese aircraft carriers destroyed by the Americans in the Battle of Midway. That was how they came to find the lone American . . ."

I couldn't believe it. None of us could. But we just kept standing there as the story kept pouring out, with Julie continuing to translate. Mr. Yamaguchi described the American, who he referred to as our "relative," and from the description we knew it had to be William Foxwell. Mr. Yamaguchi explained that the senior officers on the destroyer were angry that they had been fooled, and defeated, by the Americans. They demanded to know the location of the young sailor's aircraft carrier.

"But Mr. Yamaguchi says the American refused to tell," Julie said. "Even when a pistol was drawn by one of the senior naval officers, even under the threat of death."

Mr. Yamaguchi said he had great shame. He was afraid of his superiors. He said our relative was very brave. To the end he was very brave. A young man so brave deserved better than an anonymous burial at sea, with no record, no ceremony, nothing to mark his death.

Mr. Yamaguchi promised that he would write a formal letter to the U.S. Navy, and he would include the name Julie had given him for the young American sailor: William Foxwell. Perhaps even at this late date, honor would be restored, and William Foxwell's sacrifice could be recognized by those who loved him.

. . .

None of us moved for a couple of minutes when Julie finally hung up her phone. Greg was the first to speak, but all he could say was, "Wow."

And all I could say was, "Yeah."

And all Julie could say was, "If only he could have been here, too."

I felt that chill again, and a faint breeze, as if someone had just walked past me on the sidewalk, barely disturbing the air around me. Once again I looked to see if William Foxwell was there, and once again I didn't see him.

"You know what, you guys?" I said to Julie and Greg. "I have this feeling that he *is* here. Or he was here, anyway, standing with us the whole time Julie was talking to Mr. Yamaguchi."

Julie and Greg looked around, but, of course, nobody was there. They looked back at me expectantly.

"I know we can't see him," I said, "and I can't exactly explain it, but something just tells me William knows the rest of the story now, and that he can find the peace he's been looking for for the past seventy years."

CHAPTER 26

It was two days later, a Monday afternoon, when we met again for band practice. Some kids had made fun of us at school, just as I had predicted, but not that many. Belman kept on with the Harry Potter wisecracks and the third-grader jokes when he came over to our table at lunch, but we tried to just ignore him. There was going to be another All-Ages Open Mic Night soon, and this time we planned to be totally ready.

We had just set up our instruments and were in the middle of tuning when all of us suddenly stopped.

"Did you hear something?" I asked.

Greg nodded. "It sounds like a trumpet," he said.

"But where is it coming from?" I asked. "It was really far off, but now it almost sounds like it's right here in the room."

Julie smiled and pointed behind us. We turned around quickly and nearly fell over. It was William Foxwell!

"Hey there," he said, holding the beat-up old trumpet. "Hope I didn't scare you with my playing. I've sort of been practicing."

We all jumped up and down and shouted and stuff while he just stood there grinning. He seemed to be all there this time — no flickering or fading in and out, no faraway voice. It was like the first time he showed up in my room so many weeks ago.

"I just came to thank you again," William said when we finally quieted down. "Only this time for solving the mystery."

It was our turn to grin. "You're welcome," Greg said. "But you didn't need to thank us. We should be thanking you for everything you did in the war and all."

William might have actually blushed — it was hard to tell since he was still a ghost — and then he said he just had one more favor to ask, but it wasn't a big one.

"I was wondering if I could try to play a song with you guys," he said. "Kind of a farewell song. Before I have to go."

"Sure!" Greg said. "Anything! You name it."

"Well," William Foxwell said, holding up the trumpet again. "There was this song that was popular back when Betty and I were first going out. They used to play it on the radio. You might say it was sort of our song. Every time I ever heard it after that, I'd think about her, and she said the same thing — that it always made her think about me. So I was hoping we could play that one."

But then his face fell. "But I guess you probably wouldn't know it, now that I think about it. Heck, you probably never even heard it before."

"That's not a problem," Julie said brightly. "Tell me the name of it and I'll find it on my iPhone. We can download it from YouTube, and I can find the lyrics and arrangement for piano and the chords for guitar online, too."

William Foxwell gave her a blank look. He obviously had no idea what she was talking about.

"Never mind," Julie said quickly. "Give us a minute and we'll figure it out. Just tell me the name of the song."

William Foxwell smiled. " 'All This and Heaven Too.' "

We raced upstairs to get cell phone reception and Julie did all the things she'd told William Foxwell she would do so we could figure out how to play it. She even used Uncle Dex's printer and printed everything out for us.

"What's all this for?" Uncle Dex asked.

"No time to explain," I said, hoping that would be sufficient.

Uncle Dex shrugged and turned his attention to another customer walking into the store. "Okay," he said. "Catch you kids later."

Julie led us through the arrangement a couple of times until we sort of got it. William Foxwell joined in on the trumpet, pretty rusty at the beginning, trying to play the melody, but after a while, he got it and kept going. We followed along on our instruments, grinning at one another, not quite believing this was happening — playing music with a ghost!

It was kind of a goofy old song, the kind nobody listened to anymore, not even my parents, or probably even my grandparents. But the more we played it, the sweeter it seemed to be. I mean, still corny and all that, but it made you feel good inside. I closed my eyes and I strummed my guitar, for once not having any problem remembering the chords to a song. I don't know if Julie and Greg closed their eyes, too, but we all seemed to be in a sort of trance, playing on and on, with William Foxwell's trumpet getting stronger, and clearer, and, yes, sweeter.

And then, I realized, the song was over, and William Foxwell was gone, the trumpet lay carefully on the floor next to that old trunk where I'd found his navy peacoat and the letter to Miss Betty Corbett.

Everybody was quiet for a moment as the last haunting strains of "All This and Heaven Too" echoed in our little basement practice room — none of us quite knowing what to think, but all of us happy that William Foxwell had found his peace at last.

And then Greg asked me, "Hey, what else do you think is in that old trunk?"

AUTHOR'S NOTE

The Battle of Midway, which
took place from June 4–7, 1942, was the most important
naval battle of World War II, considered by many to be the
turning point in the fight for control of the Pacific. Six
months after the devastating Japanese attack on Pearl
Harbor, with the U.S. fleet still mostly in ruins, the Japanese
planned to attack a key U.S. air base on Midway Atoll in the
middle of the Pacific. Their intention was to lure the rest of
the American fleet from Hawaii out to defend Midway and
into what was supposed to be a final battle — with the much
smaller and vulnerable U.S. force sure to go down in defeat.

With control of Midway, and destruction of the U.S. Navy, the Japanese would then be free to launch attacks against other key Pacific islands, including Hawaii, and perhaps even the West Coast of the United States.

Instead, after breaking the Japanese radio-communication code and discovering the Imperial Navy's plan, the U.S. fleet set its own ambush. Despite overwhelming odds, they succeeded in destroying four Japanese aircraft carriers and winning a desperately needed victory in what one military historian called "the most stunning and decisive blow in the history of naval warfare." The Imperial Japanese Navy never recovered from the defeat.

Though the present-day story and characters — Anderson, Greg, Julie, their families, and William Foxwell and his friends — are fictional, all other historical events and characters in *The Secret of Midway* are real and accurate, drawn from a number of published accounts about the Battle of Midway and the brave men who fought there, far too many of whom gave up their lives defending our country.

Readers interested in learning more about the Battle of Midway, the Battle of the Coral Sea, the Japanese attack on Pearl Harbor, and the war in the Pacific can find a number of excellent sources online and in the library, just as Anderson,

Greg, and Julie did. *Miracle at Midway*, by Gordon W. Prange, with Donald M. Goldstein and Katherine V. Dillon, is a highly regarded and accessible account of the battle, with numerous sources providing both the American and Japanese perspectives. The 1976 feature film *Midway*, a blockbuster at the time of its release, contains a significant amount of actual film footage from the Battle of Midway as well.

For a sneak peek at the next

GHOSTS of WAR

adventure, turn the page . . .

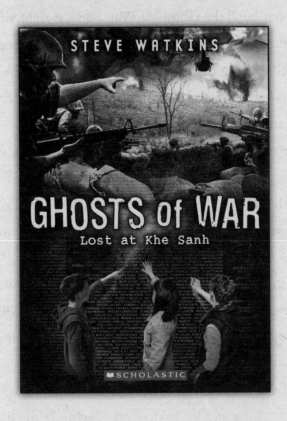

Band practice wasn't going

well — again. Two weeks after we totally stunk at the All-Ages Open Mic Night, Julie Kobayashi was still trying to convince our friend Greg Troutman that he couldn't sing, and that he *definitely* shouldn't be the front man, or front boy, for our band the Ghosts of War. She was right, of course. Once your voice starts to crack — which was exactly what happened to Greg right in the middle of our first-ever public performance — you need to step away from the microphone already and let somebody else have a turn.

The only problem — besides Greg's cracking voice — was Julie also kept trying to convince us that we should let her be the one on the mic. Unfortunately, Julie can't sing, either. Even more unfortunately, she has what my mom calls a tin ear and can't hear herself when she's singing off-key. What's even more unfortunate is she actually thinks she's a great singer. Probably since she's a musical genius in every other way, her parents never had the heart to tell her the truth — that her singing is awful times ten.

Halfway through our third song that day, with Greg still on vocals, Julie suddenly stopped playing, turned off her keyboard, and threw her hands up.

"That sounded like squeaking, not singing," she said,

before turning to me and adding, "You tell him, Anderson. He won't listen to me."

I set my guitar down and retreated to the back of our practice room in the basement of my uncle Dex's junk shop, the Kitchen Sink. No way did I want to get in the middle of those two.

Greg bent his guitar pick in half and then tried to bend it straight again. It wouldn't go. "That's just how I sing," he snapped at Julie. "It's my *style*."

"No, it's not," she snapped back. "It's your hormones."

I retreated even farther as they argued back and forth about Greg's "style," until I bumped into something. It was a footlocker. I looked down at it, confused. Just the week before I had moved it to a storage room next door to where we practiced, to get it out of the way and so I wouldn't have to see it all the time and be reminded of what was in there. I had no idea how it got back here. Maybe Uncle Dex moved it . . .

A few weeks earlier, I found a World War II navy peacoat in the locker, along with a mysterious letter, setting in motion a pretty crazy adventure involving a guy named William Foxwell — or rather the ghost of William Foxwell. Greg, Julie, and I had to solve the mystery of how he went missing in action at the Battle of Midway, which was the most important navy battle of World War II.

I wrote all about it in a notebook that I keep hidden under my mattress at home. I even gave it a title — "The Secret of Midway" — though I doubt I'll ever let anybody read it besides Julie and Greg.

Anyway, I knew there was a lot of other stuff in the locker that looked like it was from other wars, but so far I'd only glanced inside. Greg kept asking me if we could check out what was in there, but I didn't want to go messing around with anything else that might have a ghost attached to it. I was still recovering from the Secret of Midway, and missing William Foxwell, who sort of became our friend but disappeared once we solved the mystery.

It was funny about that locker, though: The more I stayed away from it, the more I couldn't stop thinking about it, like it had some kind of gravitational pull on my brain — even after I shoved it in that storage room next door. And now here it was, somehow back in the practice room.

Not only that, but as I stood there staring at it, the footlocker started to sort of glow. Then the latch fell open all on its own. Then, the next thing I knew, I was bending down without even thinking about it, opening the lid, and looking inside.

Greg and Julie were still arguing about who squeaked and who squawked when they sang, and so that's what was happening when I found the hand grenade.

I didn't know what it was at first because it was round and smooth, not like the pineapple-looking hand grenades you see in movies. More like a big olive-green lemon. Then I noticed the plunger and safety clip.

There was something written on it, too, scratched into the metal, and I had to take it closer to the front of the practice room to read what it said.

That put a quick end to Julie and Greg squabbling.

"Whoa!" Greg said. "Where did you get that?"

"You shouldn't have that," Julie said before I could answer. "It could be dangerous."

I held the hand grenade up toward the light so Greg and I could read what was on there.

The writing on the grenade said *Z & Fish* and underneath somebody had also written, or scratched, *DMZ 68*.

Greg took off his beanie, which he wore all the time because he said they made us look cool. Or at least less uncool. "What is that supposed to mean?" he asked.

"Beats me," I said. "Maybe we should take it upstairs and ask Uncle Dex."

Julie stomped her foot. "Maybe we should take ourselves upstairs and get away from that bomb before something happens," she said. She was already heading for the stairs.

"It's not a bomb, Julie," Greg said. "It's a hand grenade."

She stopped. "And what is a hand grenade, exactly?"

"Well," said Greg, pulling his beanie back on over his wild red hair, "it's, um, well, I guess it's a bomb. But you throw it. You don't shoot it out of a cannon or whatever."

"Come on," I said. "Let's all go upstairs."

"Leave it down here," Julie said again. "It could blow up and kill us. We have to get out of here."

I couldn't leave the grenade, though. It felt like my fingers were glued to it or something.

And then, as if somebody was standing right behind me, reading over my shoulder, I heard a whispery voice.

"That looks like my lucky grenade."

I whirled around and collided with Greg. Nobody else was there.

"Did you hear that just now?" I asked him.

"Heck, yeah!" he said.

We both looked around for a second, then bolted up the stairs behind Julie.

I still had the grenade.